In the sultry days of late August, a naked man is found floating near Point No Point in Lake Pepin—the only clue to his identity an odd tattoo on his shoulder.

A forty-year-old women is found shot to death in her bed, her husband Chet sobbing at her side—suicide or murder?

Deputy Sheriff Claire Watkins takes on both of the cases, the strands of which, like knotted seaweed, tangle together. Did the victims know each other? Could this connection have gotten both of them killed?

It doesn't help that Chet was Rich's best friend, which causes a rift between Claire and Rich. And as Claire's daughter Meg explores her blossoming sexuality, the summer keeps getting hotter.

In the final days of this drought summer, the temperatures continue to climb and it all boils down to what some people will do for love and sex. Claire thinks she has it figured out until she moves in closer and then, like staring at the landmark illusion of Point No Point, everything changes before her eyes.

POINT NO POINT

To Chris + Laurel —

POINT NO POINT

BY
MARY LOGUE

Mary Logue (signature)

Bleak House Books
Madison, Wisconsin

Published by
BLEAK HOUSE BOOKS
a division of Big Earth Publishing
923 Williamson St.
Madison, WI 53703
www.bleakhousebooks.com

Library of Congress Cataloging-In-Publication Data applied for.

Printed in the United States of America
12 11 10 09 08   1 2 3 4 5 6 7 8 9 10

ISBN: 978-1-60648-006-9 (Trade Cloth)
ISBN: 978-1-60648-007-6 (Trade Paper)
ISBN: 978-1-60648-008-3 (Evidence Collection)

Acknowledgments

I'd like to thank my faithful writing group: Kathy Erickson, Deborah Woodworth, Pat Boenhardt, Pete Hautman, and Bill Smith. As fast as I write, they read and tell me how to make it better. Pete gets double thanks for keeping an arm around my shoulder when the going gets tough, fabulous food on the table, and an eagle eye for the extraneous word.

As always I thank all Pepin County inhabitants. I have owned a home there for twenty years and I can't imagine my life otherwise. Special thanks to Alan and Steve at Abode Interiors for their support of my writing and artistic life, Robbi and Ted for their vegetables. Ted Johnson was invaluable help with some technical information this time around. And the Brassfields are to be thanked for helping me name a character.

Big thanks to Gerd Kreij for a wonderful, haunting photo of Lake Pepin.

Finally to the homegrown folks at Bleak House Books: Alison and Ben. I'm honored to be in their stable and delighted with the energy and enthusiasm they bring to publishing.

CHAPTER 1

Fishing for bodies was not Deputy Sheriff Claire Watkins' idea of a good time, especially during the hottest spell Wisconsin had endured this summer. In the mid-afternoon sun, Lake Pepin shimmered with the oily sheen of late August, the water a thick brew more apt to stew than refresh.

Claire sat at the bow of the Pepin County rescue launch as Deputy Bill Peterson steered the craft out of the Pepin harbor and northward, past Fort St. Antoine.

The sun came blasting down the corridor of bluffs. It felt like one hundred degrees, though she knew it couldn't be much over ninety. Even the wind blowing in her face was hot. She could hardly stand wearing her standard navy-blue polyester uniform. The dark fabric absorbed all the heat and let nothing evaporate. Sweat gathered on her chest and forehead, then ran downward.

"Hang on, going to get bumpy," Bill yelled as he cut across another boat's wake.

Claire grabbed tight to the gunnel. "I didn't know this old crate could move this fast."

Bill nodded. "Full throttle."

Up ahead she saw Point No Point, an optical illusion that had always fascinated her, a place in the river where the far bank appeared to be a wooded point jutting into the water at a sharp bend, but as you came closer the illusion faded away. There was no point, just a curve in the river. Point No Point was not a point but only a slight bulge on the shores of Lake Pepin, part of this twenty-mile section of the Mississippi River. It was a point that wasn't a point in a lake that wasn't a lake but a river. Claire loved the incongruity.

As they passed Maiden Rock, a limestone outcropping in the bluffline, she saw two boats in the water ahead waiting for them: the brand-new, fully equipped 36-foot-long water patrol boat from Lake City, which towered above the smaller 12-foot launch from Pierce County sheriff's department.

Bill slowed their boat and nosed in gently next to the other vessels. Claire immediately saw what they had been summoned to examine: the humped back of a large naked body bobbing in the water like a listing buoy. So pale and vulnerable did the fleshy broad back seem in the dark-green soup of the river that Claire felt like reaching out a hand and patting it for reassurance.

"I make it not quite two miles from the far shore," a tall, dark-haired man leaned over the railing of the Lake City patrol boat and shouted down at the other two boat crews.

"What far shore?" Ron Hansen, an officer from Pierce County, asked.

"Ours, of course. Western. Minnesota."

"Only about a quarter mile from this side," Hansen yelled back. Then he turned to Claire and Bill and said with a smirk,

"But the body is quite a ways south of the Point No Point buoy, past the 779 mile marker, which, by my estimation, puts it under the Pepin County jurisdiction."

Claire looked at the shore. She could see the mouth of a creek, its small delta jutting out into the river. "But isn't that Pine Creek over there? That's still in Pierce County."

"The county line is angled west here and cuts through the lake to up past Old Frontenac. Do you want to have a look at the Army Corps of Engineers map and see for yourself?"

Claire couldn't believe they were arguing over who got the body, none of them wanting it. They didn't even know what kind of death had occurred. The floating body could be a simple case of heart attack, or a drowning. Yes, there was a chance that it was an instance of foul play, but wasn't that their job? Yet here they were all trying to shove it off on someone else.

"I guess you'll just have to reel him in. I'd say you caught yourself a whale there," Hansen said to Claire.

It looked like Pepin County was going to get stuck with the body. Claire had to admit her heart sunk. The smallest county in Wisconsin, they were perhaps the least able to deal with the investigation this body might require. But she, too, was getting ahead of herself.

"We'll drop a buoy to mark the spot," the Pierce County deputy said.

Claire turned back to Bill.

He shrugged and said, "At least we won't have to talk about the big one that got away."

The Water Patrol Officer yelled down at them, "It's your baby. What do you want to do with it?"

Claire didn't have to think about this question. The next action might tell her what she was getting into. "Turn him over."

•   •   •

"You shouldn't be in here." Rich tried to sound stern as Meg sauntered into the kitchen, but she saw through him with no trouble. He was working at the counter, stirring something in a big yellow bowl.

"What? Is it a secret that it's my birthday? Is it a secret that you always make me a German Chocolate cake?" Meg walked up to the frosting bowl and stuck her finger into the coconutty goop. He swatted at her, but she just danced away and laughed. "Where's my mom?"

"She hasn't called, but I expect her any moment. She promised she'd be here by six. What about Curt?"

"He's coming. He said he had to milk the cows first so he might be a little later than that."

"I can't believe you're sixteen years old."

Meg could easily believe she was sixteen. She had been waiting to be that age forever. Now she could finally get her driver's license. Living out in the sticks, that meant freedom. "You know what, Rich?"

"What?"

"You've known me half my life." What she didn't add was— longer than my real dad knew me. Meg's father had died when she was six. She met Rich two years later when he started dating her mother. She guessed he was still courting Claire since, although they all lived together, Rich and Claire had not married. Which was cool with her. But sometimes she did wish Rich was her father.

"And you've known me almost a fifth of my life."

"Hey, what did you get me for my birthday?" Meg teased. "Maybe a car? That's what most kids get."

"Yup. You know the old pickup truck next to the barn?"

Meg knew the truck well. She had learned to drive the fields in that vehicle.

"That's yours, if you want it."

"Nice try. I know you've been trying to get someone to tow it away. That thing doesn't go above twenty miles an hour."

"Perfect. That's why I'm giving it to you. No reason to go faster than that," Rich said.

Meg gave him a gentle pummeling on his arm to show him she knew he was kidding. "Do you think Mom's getting me a car, a real car?"

Rich started to pour the coconut frosting on the dark cake, then stopped mid-stream to answer her question. "I think the chances of that are slimmer than the lake freezing over this afternoon."

"Right, Rich. Why don't I ever get what I really want?"

"We all wonder that." Rich chuckled.

A pounding sounded from the front door and both Meg and Rich turned to see who would walk in. Curt Hedberg nudged the door open with his foot, a huge bouquet of nodding sunflowers filling his arms. His dark hair fell over his face until he swung it back, then his smile bloomed and his eyes locked onto hers. Whenever she saw him, something opened in her heart. It just did. And then there he was—with more flowers than she knew what to do with.

"Happy sweet sixteen," Curt said, presenting her with the bouquet. "I picked them myself."

"Thank you, Curt. They're fantastic," Meg said, trying not

to get pricked by the raspy stems. She wished her mom was here to help her arrange the flowers. She put them carefully in the sink and filled it up with water to keep them wet while she found a vase.

Meg wanted her party to start right now, presents and all. "Where's Mom? It's way after six. Why isn't she here?"

"Don't worry. She'll be here any minute." Rich put the finishing touches on the frosting.

Meg was amazed at how Rich always thought the best of her mom, even if she was late a million times. "What if something comes up at work? As usual. Or what if she totally forgot?"

"Nothing would keep her from your sixteenth birthday party." Just then Rich looked out the picture window toward the lake and saw the new water patrol boat from Lake City steaming downriver and wondered who they were rescuing.

•   •   •

"I hate water," Bill Peterson said, sitting in a protective Gumby suit, scowling down at the murky surface.

Claire didn't dare laugh at the sight he made in the flame-red rubber suit, which did not complement his pale-pink skin and startling blue-green eyes. He looked like a six-foot-tall lobster.

Nor was she going to remind him that he didn't really need to wear the Gumby suit, which was more typically used in cold water. But it was the only way Bill would get in the water, especially with a dead man floating in it.

"So I've heard. I'll tie you to the boat," Claire said. "You won't drown. It'll be fine."

None of the farm boys in the deputy sheriff's office liked water. Knowing how much he disliked swimming, she had considered doing the job herself, but Bill was nearly twice as big as she was and certainly more than twice as strong. He would have to do most of the heavy lifting from the water.

Before Bill slid into the lake, Claire took a few photos, making herself look directly at the naked, severely bloated body.

The man had red hair. Other than that, he was so swollen with decomposition gasses that she had no sense of what he might have looked like, or even what size he might have been before his watery immersion. He resembled a bleached and obese fish. His face was spongy and distended, the folds of the eyelids so puffy that the eyes disappeared completely. His nose looked as if it had been chewed on. His lips were maroon and enormous, like two leeches attached to his face.

She didn't think he was anyone she knew. She sincerely hoped not. But in his present condition it was hard to tell.

A ragged hole had torn open his lower belly; the wound was now puckered around the edges. Claire saw a faded tattoo on his upper arm. That would be a huge help in identification. Especially since she could see no way the naked man could have any other form of identification on him. They'd take his fingerprints, but no guarantee they'd be on file.

Claire pointed out the wound. "Gunshot, wouldn't you say?"

Bill shrugged, then stated, "Could have been a snapping turtle. There's some really big ones, size of a garbage can lid."

"Snapping turtles. That's a good one. I guess the questions are what's he doing in the water and why is his belly ripped open, however it happened?"

"Got me. He might have floated a long ways—maybe even from the Cities. Some dangerous things go on up there."

"I wonder." Claire chewed on her lip. "Seems too far. I'm guessing he was dumped in the lake not too much upstream from here. The current just isn't that strong in this part of the lake. How many days dead do you think he is?"

"I skipped that class in forensics, but I'd guess a week at the most. He still looks human."

"An inflated human," Claire said. "Okay, Bill, enough stalling. Do you want me to give you a hand?"

With her gentle threat, Bill slowly lowered himself over the side of the boat. He clung to the edge, not wanting to let go, she guessed. She desperately wished that they had more help, but as Bill had said earlier, they'd just have to punt. There was no crime scene to protect so they might as well bring the body in themselves.

After the Pierce County deputies had realized it wasn't their body, they made a quick getaway. Then an inopportune call had taken the Lake City water patrol boat away to rescue some fishermen who had capsized. That left just Claire and Bill to manage lifting the body into their boat.

Bill wrapped a rope around the body, then tied a couple knots in it. When a gentle wave came along, he got a splash of water in his face. Claire could tell by the tightness in his face how much he hated being in the lake.

She gently pulled on the rope attached to the floater and snugged him up next to the back of the boat. What they were about to attempt to do seemed impossible—the body was literally dead weight and she wasn't sure how they were going to leverage it into the boat without tipping the whole thing over.

The boat did waver once or twice, but the whole maneuver went much more smoothly than she could have hoped: She pulled, Bill pushed and the body slid over the gunwhale and flopped into the bottom of the launch between the motor and the next seat. The sight of the engorged body up close was bad but the smell was much worse, enveloping her in a rank odor that made her gag.

Bill got to the ladder and clambered up it. "Holy Jesus! Let's get moving so we leave that stench behind."

Claire was staring at the end of the red-haired man's legs. "Look at that, Bill. What the hell happened to his ankle? It looks like it's been shredded or chewed on by something."

After pulling off the red hood of his Gumby suit, Bill looked where she was pointing. He stared at the marking around the ankle of the floating man's leg. "Really hungry snapping turtle?" he suggested.

Claire wasn't sure if it was the second mention of the snapping turtle—one of the world's ugliest creatures—the chewed-on leg, the intensely hot day, or the putrid smell, but all of sudden everything inside her was pushing out. She managed to get her head over the side of the boat before she threw up.

Bill watched her, then said just one word. "Chum."

CHAPTER 2

Claire was late, really late, and she was still a few minutes from home. She glanced at her watch again as if she could force time to slow down. But no, it was almost eight o'clock. She should have called. But there was nothing she could have told them that they didn't know—I'm running late, so sorry.

She could have said, I'm stuck in the middle of the lake with a dead body, but somehow she didn't want to tell them that over the phone. Bill had ungraciously agreed to wait for an ambulance to haul the body to the morgue or she wouldn't have gotten away even this soon.

Meg was going to be chillingly furious. Meg's birthday party. Claire's baby's birthday. No way could Meg be sixteen years old. Rich would be calm, not say much, but he would be disappointed. Meg, on the other hand, would let it out. In that respect, Meg followed in her mother's footsteps. But maybe with Curt there she would restrain herself somewhat.

Claire swung into the long driveway and stopped the squad car right in front of the house. Curt's car was parked behind Rich's. Good, he was still there. She grabbed the present she had wrapped for Meg that morning and ran into the house.

"Hey, birthday girl."

Three faces turned to look at her. Claire felt sweat pouring down her back. What was this sweating business about? She had never been so hot before in her life.

"Finally," Meg said and turned back to her plate.

"We tried to wait," Rich started to say.

"Hi, Mrs. Watkins." Curt gave her a big smile. He was a long green-bean of a kid, and cute as they come.

A huge bouquet of sunflowers sat in the middle of the table shoved down into an old canning jar. She would fix the bouquet later. No need to make Meg feel inadequate on her special day.

Claire walked up behind her daughter, dropped the present in her lap and said, "I'm sorry. The usual. Work."

"What this time?" Meg asked, without picking up the present. Claire couldn't tell how she should play this. She didn't talk a lot about her work at home, but she also didn't keep it a secret. The body floating in the lake would be written up in the paper, she was sure. They would probably need help identifying the man so the more public awareness, the better. Might as well use it and see if she could distract Meg from her poutiness. "A dead man was found floating in the lake. Right around the Point No Point buoy, but it turned out he was ours—I mean Pepin County's. No one we know. At least I don't think so. It's hard to tell because he was pretty bloated. No matter where he was killed, he was found in our jurisdiction."

"So he was killed?" Rich asked.

"Shot in the belly."

"Gross, Mom. Can't you wait until we're done eating?" Meg

said the words like they were pieces of bone she was biting down hard on.

Claire was so hungry she wanted to fall into her waiting chair and stuff the bacon, lettuce and tomato sandwich into her mouth, but even more she wanted to change clothes. The dead man's smell was still clinging to her uniform.

"I'll just be a minute."

"Want a beer?" Rich asked.

"Desperately."

"Me, too. And Curt." Meg added.

As Claire walked up the stairs, she heard Rich say, "You can split a beer. Since it's your birthday. Then cake."

Good, she hadn't missed everything.

Claire pulled off her clothes and let them fall in a puddle to the floor. Later, she promised herself. She grabbed a clean white blouse and a pair of cut-off jeans and slipped her feet into flipflops. Much better. She went into the bathroom and washed her face and hands, then washed them again, feeling like she would never get the man's decay off her skin.

Leaning into the mirror, she undid her ponytail. She was sick of her long hair. The dark hank lay on the back of her neck like an old ratty fur. Maybe it was time for a change. She was getting close to fifty, and her daughter was almost grown up.

"Mom," Meg yelled up the stairs. "We're waiting to open presents."

"Hold your horses."

"Did you get me a horse, finally?" Meg asked, with a slightly lighter tone in her voice.

Claire descended the stairs and sank into her chair—one hand grabbing the cold beer while the other clamped onto half a sandwich. The beer made it to her mouth first.

"I can open my presents now, can't I? I don't have to wait until you're done eating."

"Please, open away."

First came Rich's present. Meg ripped the wrapping off the rectangular shape with one yank and held up a mushroom identification book, the latest edition. After showing it around, Meg paged through it enthusiastically—it was a hobby the two of them shared, much to Claire's pleasure. The bounty they brought back from the woods was delicious: morels in the spring, chanterelles, boletes, and hen of the woods in the fall.

"Cool," Curt said as she handed him the book. "I'd like to learn more about mushrooms, too."

The next present was from Curt. Claire was nearly as anxious to see this as Meg. The present might give her some inside information on how serious their relationship was. As much as she liked Curt, she hated to see Meg so wrapped up in one boy. At her age she should be playing the field. However, down in Pepin County, there wasn't much of a field to play.

Curt's present was in a small box, wrapped in newsprint with red wings stamped all over it. Claire wondered if his mother was one of those women who were into stamping.

Meg tore the paper off, then waited a moment before taking the lid off. Claire hoped it wasn't too similar to what she had gotten her daughter. Then Meg opened the box and lifted out a small silver pin. Claire couldn't quite make it out. It looked like a bird.

Meg's face was filled with joy. "Curt, it's perfect," she said. "Where did you find this?"

"Online. Thought you might like it."

"What is it?" asked Rich.

Meg held it out for him to see. "It's a peregrine falcon. Our bird. You know the ones that fly off of Maiden Rock. They're special to us."

Claire held out her hand and Meg passed the pin to her. Silver bird with wings outflung. Lovely.

Meg moved on to Claire's present, also a small box. Its wrapping was also discarded quickly. Claire hoped what was inside wasn't too sentimental for her growing daughter. Meg lifted out an oval locket on a thin gold chain. "Mom, is this grandma's locket?"

"Yes, I thought it was time for you to have it."

Then Meg opened it up and looked at the two pictures that Claire had cut into the right shape to fit inside the frames. One was a photo of Steven, her father, holding Meg when she was just born. The other was Rich and Claire, hugging. Her parents. All three of them.

As Claire watched tears fill Meg's eyes, she guessed she had done okay.

"Mom, this is just what I wanted, even though I didn't know it. Thank you." She came to her mother and gave her a big hug. Even kissed her on the head. What more could a mother ask for?

"What I thought I wanted was a new Prius," Meg said as she went to sit back down. "Silly me."

Rich pushed back from the table and said, "How 'bout some cake? Claire, are you sticking around or do you have a date with a dead man?"

"Nope, I asked Amy to sit in with the medical examiner. I'm done for the night."

All three pair of eyes turned to look at her.

"Mom, for real? You're letting someone else do something?" Meg asked, incredulous.

Rich gave Claire a good-for-you look.

• • •

Medical examiner Janet Davis' green rubber gloved finger tapped the rib cage of the opened torso as she explained, "Water gets into the lungs one of two speeds: slow or fast."

This was Deputy Sheriff Amy Schroeder's first time attending an autopsy on her own. She had watched a couple with Claire Watkins and had always found them a challenge. For one thing, the morgue was a long narrow room with no windows in the basement of the hospital, which kept in the dank and a disturbing vinegary smell that she never wanted to pull too deeply into her lungs. The shallow breathing she was forced to do didn't help her feel very comfortable.

Amy didn't know whether she should laugh or not at Janet's comment. But she decided what the heck. After all, the guy was dead. She let out a small chuckle. "Wow. These technical terms. What do you mean—slow or fast?"

"Well, if you must have technical terms," Janet said, snapping the green rubber glove, "How about the difference between gooshing or seeping?"

"What we want to know for starters is, was he dead when he hit the water?" Amy knew this was the first thing that Claire would ask her.

Janet peered into the gaping chest cavity. A small woman,

she needed to stand on her tiptoes for some of the work she did. "I would have to say, yes, from what I can gather, he was already dead. Although there is water in his lungs, I think that it seeped in during his long immersion in the lake. The technical term we use to describe this process is infiltration."

"It's going to be tough to identify this guy. Any birthmarks?" Amy asked.

"He's got an odd mole here on his rib cage. But I'm not sure that anyone would notice it. Even his mother or wife. But then there's the tattoo," Janet pointed at the dark mark on his shoulder.

"Great. A tattoo is perfect. What is it?"

"Well, I think I know, but come here and look yourself. Tell me what you think it is."

Amy walked around the steel table and bent over to get a better look at the tattoo. Janet turned the light on it. The tattoo was dark. It seemed to be done in only one color, but hard to tell what color it was, blue or brown or black. Then she decided it was green. But the shape looked like an hour glass: large, then small, then large again. Suddenly the image came into focus and she saw what it was: branches, trunk, roots. "I think it's a tree."

"Yeah, that's what I was guessing too. Unusual for a big burly guy to have a tree tattooed on his shoulder. I've never seen one before, but this new crop of guys getting tattooed aren't going for the usual mermaids and eagles. I'm seeing more dragons and, believe it or not, swallows. So a tree might be perfectly usual."

"While the tree won't help us find him, like a navy insignia would, it certainly will help us make a positive identification when it comes to that." Amy's eyes strayed down his body. "Any chance you can tell me what happened to his ankle? I told you what Bill said about it."

Again Janet looked at the mentioned body part even though all that was left of it was bone. "Not a snapping turtle, as your compatriot suggested. I'd say something was tied around it, probably attached to some kind of weight. Look here." Her green rubberized finger pointed at the edge of skin over the ankle bone.

Amy leaned in, trying not to breathe. She could see the skin looked stretched at the edges, worn through to the bone in places.

The medical examiner continued. "I'm guessing somebody didn't want this body to be found."

●   ●   ●

Rich smelled Claire's wet, sweet hair as she lay drowsing next to him. She must have been beat, because she asked him to keep a watch out for Meg and then fell right to sleep. It was nearly midnight—Meg's birthday curfew. The book he was reading wasn't bad, but he kept losing his place and staring off into space. He felt restless and not particularly sleepy.

The phone rang. The real phone, not Claire's work cell-phone. Rich grabbed it before it could ring again and wake up Claire. He assumed it was Meg with some explanation as to why she couldn't make it home in the next five minutes. Even though it was her birthday, he was going to have to be strict with her. Claire thought that he was way too lenient with Meg. He just found it hard to say no to her, and she didn't ask for much.

"Hello," he said quietly as he slid out of bed and headed toward the bedroom door so he wouldn't wake up Claire.

At first there was no sound, then heavy breathing rasped on the other end of the phone line.

"I think you've got the wrong number," Rich said once he stepped out into the hallway and closed the bedroom door. He was ready to read whoever was on the other end the riot act. How stupid do you have to be to call a deputy sheriff's number and make an obscene phone call?

"Rich," a deep male voice gasped.

He recognized the voice immediately. His old friend, Chet Baldwin. Hadn't heard from him in a while. What was he doing calling so late? "Chet?"

"Rich, I need some help." Chet's voice sounded awful, like someone had shot it full of holes. He was wheezing and breathing hard.

"What's going on, Chet? Are you okay?"

"No, I just don't know." Then he started to cry, a sound like wood being torn into shreds. Awful.

Rich had never heard Chet cry before, in all their many years of being friends, really since grade school. They had played softball together. Chet had been a hell of a pitcher. Even the time that Chet got slammed in the face by a solid hit by Sammy Schultz and it broke his cheek bone, even then he hadn't cried.

"Chet, what's the matter? Tell me what's going on."

Chet managed to say, "I don't know what to do. It's just a big mess over here. Could you come over?"

"Isn't Anne there?" Rich asked.

Chet had married about ten years ago to a younger

woman—about fifteen years younger than Chet's fifty-five years. Chet had met Anne at a square dance in Red Wing, Minnesota. She had danced him off his feet and vice versa.

Chet started to cry. "She's part of the problem."

"Anne?" Rich asked. But who else could the "she" be? They had no children. At least none that Rich knew of. Chet's mother had died years ago. As far as Rich knew there was no other woman in Chet's life but Anne.

"Yes. I don't know how it happened."

Rich hadn't heard anything about Anne being sick. In fact, he had seen her a few weeks ago when the woodcarvers had met over at Chet's house. She had looked lovely and seemed in good spirits. "Is she okay?"

"I don't know. I was gone. Went for a walk."

"Chet, has there been an accident?"

"I can't say it." Chet's voice was growing fainter as if he were holding the phone farther away from his mouth.

"What happened, Chet?"

Muffled sounds. Rich couldn't tell if Chet was crying or if he was trying to say something.

"Talk to me," Rich gripped the receiver hard.

"This is too hard. I don't know what I'm going to do." Chet finally replied. "I need you, buddy."

CHAPTER 3

I have to go," Meg said, gently extricating herself from Curt's arms, legs, and mouth.

"You don't want a little more of your birthday present?" he asked her, touching the side of her face.

She felt her innards start to quiver, but didn't give in.

Meg kissed him and let that be her answer, however he would take it, but she didn't fall back into his arms. "Hey, they're just starting to trust us again. I don't want to ruin that."

Curt nodded his head. Meg knew he understood. For the first few months of their relationship, Meg had been under house arrest after a friend of theirs had died under dubious circumstances. It had taken Claire and Rich many trial at-home dates to feel okay about the two of them going any place together. Meg wasn't about to go backwards.

"It's almost time," she said, while adjusting her clothes. They weren't far from her house. She'd be home pretty close to her curfew.

Curt leaned in close to her, held her eyes, and announced in a clear voice, "I love you."

Meg dropped her eyes and stammered, "You do?"

"Sure. It's easy."

Meg knew she couldn't leave his declaration unanswered. "Curt, I think I love you too."

Curt laughed and rubbed her head. "That's your problem. You think too much, my Meglet."

"Well, I wasn't prepared."

"What's there to be prepared about?" he asked, sounding put out, his voice deeper than usual.

"I don't know. I've always thought of it as a special kind of moment. I could have used more time, you know, to think about how to do it right. I figured we'd discuss it or something, like we do everything."

"Hey, it's your birthday. I'd call that a special moment." Curt pulled away from her and sounded mad. "Plus, we've been seeing each other for almost a year. I don't think I'm saying anything rash."

"No, you're right."

"I'm not asking you to marry me," he said, sounding even a little more put out.

"I hope not." Marriage, she hoped with anyone, was a good ten years off.

"Why? Wouldn't you?" Curt pulled back from her.

"Curt, you know what I mean. Not now." Meg knew she had to make it up to him. "But that was really nice to hear and especially on my birthday." She touched the peregrine falcon pin that she was wearing on the collar of her shirt. "You're the best boyfriend a girl could ever have."

Curt seemed somewhat appeased as he started the car. "I'll get you home before you turn into a pumpkin."

"I'm not the pumpkin. But your clunky vehicle might turn into a vegetable at any moment."

"First I can't say I love you and now you're picking on my car." Curt drove out of the wayside rest.

"No, I just meant, wrong allusion. It isn't Cinderella who turns into the pumpkin, it's her carriage."

"Well, I guess it's wrong all the way around. I know you can't be Cinderella, cuz I'm obviously not Prince Charming."

Meg giggled. "No, you're more like the Prince Symbolina."

Curt started singing "Purple Rain" at the top of his lungs, a not entirely unpleasant sound, although his falsetto sounded mainly like screeching. If he hadn't been driving, Meg would have kissed him to make him stop.

When they pulled into the farm's driveway, Meg was surprised to see the outside lights were on. Then her mom came out the door with Rich right behind her. She had hoped they'd be in bed.

Geez, Meg thought, they really don't trust me yet. They've been waiting up and now they're the welcoming party.

But as she got out of the car, she could hear them talking and it wasn't about her curfew.

"He called me. I don't know what's happened over there. He sounded terrible. That's all I know. I'm going over there." Rich sounded upset.

Rich was rarely upset. Usually at machines that didn't work. Meg wondered what they were talking about.

"Rich, do you want me to come with you?" Claire said back in a low and steady voice. "If something bad's happened, maybe I should come along."

"I got the feeling that Anne has left him. He didn't come right out and say it, but that's my feeling. In which case, it'd be better if you weren't there."

Meg could tell that comment got to Claire as her voice lifted and intensified. "Okay, just thought I'd offer."

"Much appreciated."

Meg looked at Curt, who was standing next to the car. He shrugged. Meg thought it might be wise to just slip into the house. She quickly gave Curt a light good night kiss and motioned him back into the car. He followed her cue and backed out of the driveway.

"Hi, I'm home," Meg said as she walked to the deck where her mom and Rich were standing.

"Hey, honey. You have a nice time?" her mother said, squeezing her shoulders.

"Yeah, we just hung out. Nothing much to do around here. What's going on, Mom?" Meg asked, curious how much they'd tell her. Who would need Rich in the middle of the night?

"Just something Rich needs to check on."

Rich spoke up. "It's just Chet, Meg. He's having a hard time and asked me to come over. Not sure what it's about."

With her arm still around Meg's shoulders, Claire started to walk into the house, then turned back to Rich. "Call me and let me know what's going on if you have a chance."

•   •   •

Rich felt like he had known Chet Baldwin all his life. In fact, they had met when they were five years old.

One of Rich's earliest memories of Chet was sitting next to him in the lunch room. Rich had been so impressed because for lunch Chet had two hard-boiled eggs and a store-bought set of miniature salt and pepper shakers. He thought that little set was one of the coolest things he had ever seen. He asked Chet if he could use them and Chet had been rather hesitant to hand them over, but finally he did, carefully supervising the amount of salt that Rich had sprinkled on his sandwich.

"You know, salt makes you strong," Chet had said. "Really?" Rich had asked. "Yup, that's what my grandpa told me. Comes from the ocean. So I eat a lot of salt." Later at home, when Rich's mom had noticed him dumping salt into his hand and licking it, she asked him why he was doing that. He had explained and she had laughed at him. All she had said was, "A little goes a long way. As they say, I'd take what Chet Baldwin tells you with a grain of salt." Then she laughed again.

Rich had taken his mother's advice and often tempered what Chet said. He knew that Chet exaggerated when he thought it would make the story better, but Rich had never known him to lie.

When Rich reached the Baldwin home, the front door was standing wide open and most of the lights were on. Rich stepped into the living room and saw no one. He heard nothing. No television, or radio. No talking. No noise of anyone moving around anywhere.

This silence bothered him more than a screaming fight would have. Where was everyone?

He hollered, "Chet?"

No answer.

Rich took another step or two into the living room and then stopped to look around. Growing up, he had spent a lot of time in this house. Chet had lived in it his whole life. The living room had always struck him as a pleasant, cozy place where you could settle in to read and think. An old iron wood-stove was its centerpiece, with a faded couch that was long enough to stretch out on and a set of matching Amish rocking chairs. The Red Wing newspaper was spread out on the coffee table, but other than that, everything seemed in its place.

He went to the hallway. "Where are you?"

Still no answer, but Rich thought he heard a noise. He followed it.

Pushing the bedroom door open, he stood back and looked in.

A lamp glowed on the bedside table. Two people were lying on the bed. At first glance, an intimate scene: the woman was stretched out straight and the man was curled up next to her. Anne and Chet Baldwin. Anne was wearing a sheer nightgown. She was a lovely woman and her form showed through the gauzy material just as it was meant to.

But there was a dark hole in the middle of her forehead and a red halo around her head as if someone had painted it on the pink-flowered bedspread.

Chet was so still that for a moment, Rich worried that his friend might be dead too. Then he heard a whisper of a cry.

Rich stepped back from the doorway and walked down the hallway. This was as bad as it gets. He found the phone in the kitchen and called Claire. She answered on the first ring and when he said, "Get over here," she didn't ask any questions. She just said, "I'm coming."

When Rich went back to the bedroom, he found Chet clutching Anne's right arm and softly keening. Something dark was smeared on his hands and on his face.

"Chet, we need to get you out of here." Rich stepped toward him, but stopped a few feet from the bed.

Chet didn't respond to him.

"Chet, Claire's coming over now. You need to pull it together. Get off the bed." Rich forced himself to reach down and put his hand on his friend's shoulder. At his touch, Chet turned his head toward Rich and looked at him as if he was trying to place him.

"Come on, Chet. Get up."

"I can't leave her," Chet whispered.

"Just get off the bed. It'll be all right. We'll stay right here."

"You won't make me leave her?"

"No," Rich took Chet's arm and got him to sit on the edge of the bed. "What happened here, buddy?"

Whatever had happened that night had aged Chet a good twenty years. His gray hair was sodden with sweat, his skin sallow and collapsed in on his face. He looked feverish and weak from the force of the recent trauma.

Chet glanced at Rich, his eyes uneasy and twitchy, and then turned back to his wife. "Anne's gone."

Rich didn't know what more to say. He didn't want to ask any questions for fear of what Chet might say. He kneeled down by the bed and mourned whatever had happened to Anne.

Fifteen minutes later, he heard someone at the front so he yelled, "Claire, back here. In the bedroom."

She stepped cautiously into the room and stopped when she saw Rich kneeling by Chet. "Oh." The sound whistled out of her like a soft scream.

She took a step closer, scanning the scene, then focusing on Anne's still body. "Is she dead? Is he okay? Who shot her?"

Before Rich could answer her, Chet stood up as if he was about to say something, but no words came out.

The gun he'd been cradling fell to the floor with a thud.

•   •   •

Claire slipped her hand into the pocket of her uniform and pulled on a pair of rubber gloves before she bent down and picked up the gun, not sure of the make, but noting that it was a .38 revolver, a nice little pistol that was especially effective at close range, didn't tend to send bullets through walls.

"Is this your gun, Chet?" She asked an easy question, trying to get him ready to talk. Chet had a full arsenal of firearms. He was known to be a hunter and an excellent marksman; he often gave them venison in the fall.

"No, it was Anne's," he said with his head sunk down between his shoulders. He looked as if he would topple over. Rich stood right next to him, ready to catch his friend if he passed out. "I bought it for her on her birthday two years ago. I taught her how to use it. She named it after Annie Oakley. Called it Oakley."

His answer jolted her at first, but then it made sense. So it was Anne's gun, possibly kept in the bedside table drawer in case of an intruder. "Let's get you out of here. I need to make a couple calls."

"There's a phone in the kitchen," Chet said as he followed her out of the room. Rich walked right next to him.

Claire called in to the dispatcher and asked that whoever was on hand be sent out to the Baldwin house. Then she turned her attention back to Chet. "I'm going to be asking you some questions now and I'm going to be asking them as a deputy sheriff. You understand."

He lifted up his head slowly as if it weighed almost too much for his neck to carry. "Yes, Claire, I do."

She had to stop herself from moving in on him and giving him a consoling hug. Sorrow radiated off of him in waves. "These questions might seem scary, but that's just what I have to do. Try to answer them as best you can. Do you understand?"

"Claire," Rich started to say, but she shot him a dirty look.

"Do you understand, Chet?" she asked again.

Rich said slowly and clearly, barely controlling his anger. "Give the guy a break, Claire. His wife is dead. He's in shock. Let's get him something to drink."

"This is not a social visit. What happened here tonight?" Claire asked Chet, wishing somehow that she could get Rich out of this house. She tried to send him a thought dagger or two, but his ESP seemed not to be working, or he was totally ignoring her. He moved in closer to Chet as if to protect his friend from Claire's questions. "How did the gun go off?"

Chet bowed his head and shook it back and forth.

Rich put an arm on his friend's shoulder and said, "Let's all go and sit down. Chet will tell us what happened here. He didn't do anything to his wife, for god's sake, he's on the county board."

"What does that have to do with anything?" Claire asked.

"You know what I'm trying to say, Claire. He's a good person," Rich said.

Claire felt like another person had stepped into her body. A very angry woman was taking over. "Rich, you need to back off. It's my job to ask Chet whatever I need to in order to understand what took place in this room. For god's sake, a dead woman is lying on the bed. Now, you either shut up or get out of here. But Chet needs to answer some questions right now."

Rich grabbed Chet's arm and turned the dazed man so he was no longer facing toward Claire. He spoke quietly. "Chet, you don't need to say anything right now. Take your time."

"I don't mind answering some questions. Claire's got a right to know. It's her job," Chet said. He turned back toward Claire.

"What happened tonight?" Claire asked.

"We had a fight," Chet started, then sagged more. "You know, we never fought. In all our ten years together. I mean, maybe over the laundry or something stupid, but this was a real fight. All my fault."

"What were you fighting about?"

Chet shook his head, didn't answer.

"Did the gun go off during this fight?" Claire asked.

"No, not then."

"When?"

Chet lifted his head again as if he were coming up for air. "Well, I went for a walk after the fight. I needed to get out of here. It must have happened sometime after I left and before I got back."

"How long were you gone?"

"About an hour or so, I'd guess."

"Can anyone confirm that you went for a walk?" Claire asked. "Did you see anyone?"

"Just Bentley."

Claire felt hopeful.

Then he added, "Anne's dog."

CHAPTER 4

Amy parked her squad car behind Claire's. She sat for a moment and drank the dregs of her coffee. It was after two in the morning. All she wanted to do was lean her head forward onto the steering wheel, close her eyes, and go away. Just her luck that Claire's call had caught her as she was finishing up with the medical examiner. Another minute or two and she would have been out the door, on her way home to a beer, an hour of late-night TV, and some much needed sleep.

But Claire had said there had been a shooting and they needed to secure the premises and call in reinforcements. It wasn't a drill they went through very often and Amy would rather not miss it.

Pepin County had been very quiet since the meth bust they had a year or so ago. Just the usual toilet-paperings, drunk drivers, dead deer, and motorcycle accidents. In the two years since Amy had joined the department, motorcycle accidents had increased in the county by fifty percent.

All these old geezers were trying for a second teenage-hood by buying the Harleys they couldn't afford when they were seventeen. Some of them weren't living to talk about it. They had discovered how fun it was to drive along the shore of Lake Pepin and through the bluffs of Pepin County, disturbing the locals with their loud tailpipes, scaring the livestock, and not always being able to avoid either the wildlife or each other. Bad things happened to people when they flew off bikes at high speeds, or even low. Things she wished she hadn't seen: limbs severed, skin torn away to bone, head trauma so bad that the skull appeared to have the fragility of an eggshell.

Amy stepped out of the car and threw that last bitter sip of coffee onto the ground, then tossed her mug back onto the seat of her car. The air was still warm and very humid, making it feel like she was in a sauna. She could smell some flower blooming, but didn't know enough to identify the cloyingly sweet smell. The lights in the house were on.

All Claire had said was there had been a shooting and a woman was dead, her husband near hysterical. Amy wondered what she would find inside.

• • •

Rich watched in dismay as Claire gave Amy the job of babysitting Chet. As if she didn't even trust him to take care of his friend. She left the three of them sitting at the kitchen table: chunky, blond Amy who was valiantly trying to stay awake; Chet, who would sit silently for a while and then talk non-stop as if he could scramble back in time if he worked hard enough; and Rich, who was wondering what the hell was going on with Claire.

Rich had never seen her like this before. She was acting as if he was infringing on her territory, and she was being mean about it. The meanness was the part that concerned him.

More deputies entered the house, some of them sticking their heads into the kitchen and giving the nod to him and Amy. Bill Peterson came in and rubbed Amy's shoulders for a second. At first, Rich was surprised, then he remembered that Claire had told him that the two deputies were seeing each other socially. No one said anything to Chet even though a few of the deputies knew him.

Suddenly Chet started talking, launching into the middle of a conversation. "Did I ever tell you about the first time I saw Anne?"

Rich knew the story well, the tale of a dance where Chet had met Anne, but he shook his head because he knew Chet needed to tell this, needed to have Anne alive for a moment again.

"I didn't usually go to those things, those square dances. You know me, Rich. I'm not that kind of a guy. Dancing reminds me of someone having an epileptic fit. So it was weird that I would go to this dance. I think I was just killing time. But I went and I stood against the wall and I watched all these people promenading around the room in these crazy outfits, women in turquoise skirts all puffed out like upside-down petunias. And most of them knew exactly what they were doing, like precision dancing, do-se-doing when they were supposed to, alamanding left and the whole nine yards."

Chet stopped talking and his tongue strayed out to his dry lips and Rich knew he was back there, could smell the sweat off the swirling dancers.

"Anyways, then I saw her. She was wearing a pair of jeans and some kind of shirt. She didn't know when to do-se-do or promenade, but as she got swinging and her blond hair was flying, she was just having so much fun—she was having the time of her life." He paused again. "I knew I wanted in."

Rich nodded.

Chet continued, "We got married three months later. You remember. I think I surprised myself, I surprised everyone. Confirmed bachelor. That was awful fast, but I knew that she was the one. You know how you know."

Amy lifted her chin up from the cup of her hands. "How do you know?"

"When they make you want to live more than you ever have before. Besides, she was a hell of a cook." Chet's eyes filled up. "She made Reuben sandwiches last night with potato salad. She knows how much I like her potato salad."

Rich thought about the meal he had made for the birthday party earlier that evening. He couldn't believe that was only a few hours ago. He wondered if Claire had appreciated it; if she appreciated what he did for her anymore. It seemed like she took him for granted and then she yelled at him when he wanted to help out his old friend.

"Chet, you want me to stay here tonight?"

Chet shook his head. "No need for that, Rich. It won't matter. I don't really care what happens any more. I deserve it all."

Rich couldn't believe he heard Chet say that. Even though he was afraid to hear the answer, he couldn't help but asking, "What d'you mean?"

"What more can they do to me? I lost the love of my life. My beautiful Anne. Not much else matters."

"Chet, you've got to take care of yourself. You might think

about calling a lawyer before you talk to Claire. This is serious."

Claire stepped into the room, but didn't look at Rich.

He hoped she hadn't heard what he had just said to Chet. She would claim he was interfering again. All he was doing was being a friend to Chet.

"Amy, could you go back and help Speedo with the photos? Just make sure he takes shots from all angles. And then if you would watch the body until it gets moved to the morgue. Then head home. I know you're working way past your shift. I'm going to take Chet back to the department with me."

Chet bent his head over.

Claire turned to Rich, "Before you say anything, I'm taking him in because I need to talk to him and find out what happened here. He can't stay here, obviously. Won't hurt him to stay in the jail overnight. He can talk to whoever he wants in the morning. I'll make sure of that."

Rich decided not to argue with her.

Chet looked up at Rich. "Could you feed Bentley and see that the horses get let out to pasture in the morning?"

"Sure, Chet."

"Can't let anything happen to Bentley. Anne loved that damn dog almost as much as she loved me."

• • •

A deep, dark moonless night was all around them as Claire headed away from the river and up Highway 25 toward Durand. Good thing she knew this road so well. It was lightly lit by the squad car headlights, one of which seemed to be turned a little high and slanted off to the right, catching the edge of the corn fields. She kept her eyes sharp for animals running across the road. Deer were the biggest problem. They could total a car, but she even hated to hit raccoons or possums.

Chet sat next to her in the squad car—she had seen no reason to put him in the back, even though it was procedure—and stared straight ahead as they drove through the night down Highway 25. On the best of days, Chet wasn't chatty, and tonight he wasn't saying a word. Claire wasn't sure what to make of his silence. She wanted to give him beyond the benefit of a doubt, but it was hard given what she had seen at his house.

As much as she hated to admit it, she was betting that Chet had killed his wife, but—knowing too how in love they had been, having seen them together for many years and never having witnessed a mean word between them—she hadn't a clue as to why. But at the moment he was the only suspect. And, from her long years of working homicide, she knew that people were most often killed by family, by their loved ones.

At the moment, she just wanted to get him to the jail, do a gunpowder residue test on his hands to document that he had held the gun, and put him to bed. She had to remember to ask the medical examiner to do a similar test on Anne. Maybe, when they got the results of these two tests, it would be clear what happened.

It was nearly three o'clock in the morning and Claire was starting to seriously fade, feeling a tiredness that no caffeine could alleviate. She was afraid she was in no shape to drive home. She might just sleep at the jail herself—there was a bunk that sheriff's personnel could use.

Most people were killed at night. It made sense—most murders involved drinking—but the older she got the harder it was for her to work so late. It didn't appear that either Chet or Anne had been drinking, although she knew they enjoyed a bottle of beer and a glass of wine as much as the next person. Even though Chet said they had argued, there had been no signs of struggle anywhere in the house.

From her many long years of seeing such crime scenes, Claire was convinced that Anne had been killed by someone else's hand, probably her husband's, and that she had not suicided. Two concrete facts steered her thinking in that direction: First, there had been no suicide note. Claire had looked hard— under the pillows, in the bedside tables, in Chet's office and even in the kitchen before they left the house—maybe one would turn up but she doubted it. Such notes weren't usually hidden.

The second fact was that Anne hadn't died in the bed. She had died, probably standing up, in the middle of the living room. Claire had found a large blood stain on the oriental rug. It had been hard to see at first because of the matching dark red color of much of the intricate pattern of the wool rug, but Claire had taken a Kleenex and pressed it into the fabric and it pulled out a smear of fresh red liquid, most certainly blood. Then there was the hole in the middle of the forehead, most suicides shot themselves in the temple.

Women who killed themselves almost always left a note trying to explain their actions—weren't women always trying to explain themselves?—and usually killed themselves lying down in bed, not standing in the middle of the living room.

All this lessened the possibility that Anne had killed herself. And if someone else killed her, Chet was the only suspect.

Then there was Chet's behavior. She had seen enough killers when she worked in Minneapolis to know how some of them reacted in the aftermath of a murder they had committed. They were capable of a disassembling, grieving the death as if they had had nothing to do with it. In many cases their sorrow was real. Appalled at what they had done, wishing they could undo it, they were not acting when they cried and mourned their victim's passing. But, like Chet, they rarely offered a good explanation for what had happened.

Chet had not mentioned one reason why Anne might have killed herself. Not suggested one reason for her having committed such a desperate act. Or suggested any other person who might be responsible.

So, while Claire was sure that Chet had deeply loved Anne and was terribly sad that she had died, distraught to the point of being speechless, she was afraid that he had pulled the trigger on the gun that had shot his wife.

How would she explain this all to Rich? Maybe she wouldn't have to. Maybe he would settle down and as the facts came out, know that she was just doing her job. Best yet would be if Chet would confess. At the moment she wasn't hopeful that would happen any time soon.

Claire remembered a barbecue earlier in the summer over at the Baldwin's. Rich and Chet had been playing horseshoes. Anne and Claire had sat at the picnic table and watched the two men out in the field. They were drinking gin and tonics and

Claire remembered thinking what a perfect drink for a mid-summer evening—tart and thirst-quenching.

Bentley sat right next to Anne, his head taking up her whole lap. Her hand played with his ears. "What does he want?"

"The dog?"

Anne laughed. "Oh I know what he wants. He's easy to please. No, I meant my husband."

For some reason, Claire hadn't pursued it. The question had sat between them. Soon it got too dark to see and the men joined them in the gloaming.

Claire thought back on that scene and wondered what Anne had meant, what Chet had been up to.

As if he were reading her mind, Chet asked, "Aren't you going to ask me if I killed Anne?"

"Yes. At some point I will ask you that."

"What if I tell you I didn't? Would you take me back home?"

"No, Chet, I think you need to stay with us at least overnight." Claire followed the car beams down the road. "What I want to know is why in the hell did you move her?"

"How'd you know that?"

"Found the blood on the carpet."

"I couldn't leave her lying in the middle of the floor. On the carpet. It didn't seem right. She looked so cold. I just thought she'd be more comfortable in the bed, you know."

Disassembling. "It looks bad that you moved her, Chet. Kind of suspicious." As long as he was talking, she might as well ask him the big question. If she got him to answer it, Claire was sure he wouldn't change his story. "All right. So, tell me, did you kill her?"

"I might as well have." He didn't say another word the rest of the ride.

CHAPTER 5

In what seemed like only minutes after Claire put her head down on the hard little pillow on the hard little cot in the jail's spare room, she was being woken up by someone shaking her: the new deputy, red-eared and pimple-faced but nice Jeremy, who was saying, "Sheriff told me to wake you."

Claire sat up, glad she had not bothered to strip out of her uniform, and tried to figure out what was going on and why Jeremy was shaking her. "What's the matter, Jer?"

The new deputy was wringing his hands and nodding toward the hallway. "He hung himself with the sheet. You gotta come."

"Who? What are you talking about?"

"That guy that shot his wife."

Chet. Claire bolted upright and asked, "Where is he?"

"The sheriff and Red are there. They're administering CPR. Sheriff told me to wake you."

"Fine, Jeremy. That's fine." Claire stumbled to the doorway and looked down the hall to where she had left Chet a few hours ago. She could hardly walk straight, her body listing from sleeplessness to one side, her eyes gummed with sleep. "What time is it anyway?"

"Seven-thirty."

Just as she started to walk toward Chet's cell, the door at the end of the hallway burst open and a group of EMTs boiled down the corridor, with a gurney in tow. She stopped and watched them turn into the room, then came up behind them.

The room was filled with action, which was a good sign. That meant they were still trying. There was hope for Chet. As the EMTs worked on him, Claire could see his crumpled body on the floor at the foot of his cot, a tangled scarf of a sheet stretched out behind him, his head turned to one side, an oxygen mask strapped on, his eyes closed. Was he breathing? She couldn't tell.

Something in Claire began to crumble. She remembered going over to Chet and Anne's for a big venison dinner after hunting season last year. Rich had made stuffing with hen of the woods, she had found the time to make an apple pie with what was left of the fall fruits. The four of them had sat around the bountiful table and eaten and drank and laughed until their eyes were full of tears.

Why hadn't she sat up all night and talked to Chet until he explained exactly what had happened? Why hadn't she had him sedated so there was no chance of him waking and trying anything? She blamed herself for what had happened. But she had not thought he was suicidal. Plus, she knew he would be checked on hourly by the wardens.

Maybe she should have left him at home to take care of his animals. She shook her head. Then he might really be dead. Full access to guns and pills and no one to check on him.

"We've got a pulse," one of the EMTs said. "Let's get him out of here."

They moved him onto a neck board, hoisted him up onto the gurney, and rolled him down the hall and out the door.

Then they were gone, Red following behind. The quiet they left behind was disturbing. Claire, Sheriff Talbert, and Jeremy looked at each other.

"Fill me in here, Claire. What was Chet doing here? Was he under arrest?" the sheriff asked.

"Not really. Not yet. I just didn't want him to be left alone in the house and I wanted to question him first thing in the morning."

"You think he killed his wife?"

Claire wanted to be careful with what she said to the sheriff. This was a small county. The sheriff was close friends with Chet too. She needed to work the crime scene and find out what story would be revealed in the blood and fingerprints and bullet hole.

"To tell you the truth, I'm not sure what happened." She filled him in on what they had found at the Baldwin's house.

The sheriff gave Claire an up-and-down scan. She was sure the bright lights and little sleep weren't showing her at her best either. "I guess we'll just have to see what happens. Why don't you go back and try to catch a few more hours of sleep. I know what time you got here last night. I fear it's going to be a long day."

Claire watched the face of the man she had worked with for many years and trusted. The light in the jail cell and the early morning didn't do much for the sheriff's pallor. He looked older than usual.

Claire said, "Stewey, I'll say this—it doesn't look good. What do you think? You know him pretty well. Could Chet do such a thing?"

Sheriff shook his head as if to rid it of his own dark thoughts. "Chet was a proud man. Never knew him to be violent. Who knows what any of us can do when we get pushed. But I can't imagine what it would take to push Chet that hard."

•   •   •

When Meg came downstairs in her long purple t-shirt that she wore as a nightie, the first thing she asked was, "Where's Mom?"

Rich knew he couldn't talk about what he had seen last night so he just said, "Work."

This one word was enough explanation for Meg. She grabbed the Frosted Flakes out of the cupboard, the milk out of the fridge, and poured herself a cup of coffee. This was new for her this summer. She had just started drinking coffee. Rich was sure she thought it made her seem more grown-up. But then she put three teaspoons of sugar and a hefty slug of milk into it until the brew turned the color of chocolate milk, which rather ruined the adult effect.

Rich stood by the counter and blew on his own cup of real black coffee and tried not to think about Chet. He hadn't slept well or long and he felt really shaky. Chet was a very close friend and his wife had died of a gunshot wound. He couldn't get the image of the two of them on the bed together out of his mind.

But there was even more than that to what he was feeling. He had a horrible gut feeling that Claire was gunning for Chet. She had turned very cop at the scene and then had closed down about what she was thinking, but he could see it in her face when she looked at Chet. She thought he had killed his wife. And something about Claire thinking that kicked a hole in Rich's guts. How could she think that of one of his best friends? What did that say about her?

Meg poured milk onto her cereal and then hit it with the back of her spoon to sink the floating cereal pieces. "Did she even come home last night?"

"No," Rich answered.

• • •

"You're her favorite," Bill said, leaning over Amy's desk. "You girls have to hang together."

Amy ran her finger down the scar on her face, then quickly pulled her hand away. It was a bad habit she was trying to quit. The scar was nearly impossible to notice on her face, but she could still feel it, a tightness like a puckering where it sat on her cheekbone.

"She doesn't have favorites. And we're not girls. I just happened to be there. That's all. That's why she asked me to watch and report on the medical examiner's findings. Could have been anyone," Amy said as she looked up into his big smiling face. He had a dimple in his left cheek. She wanted to reach up and poke it with her finger, but she tried to resist touching him during work. "You could have done it, Bill, but you left. You went home right at the end of your shift, like you always do. Anyways, you don't like looking at dead bodies."

"You got that right. The less I have to be in the morgue the better I like it. Give me drunks any day over dead bodies, especially Mr. Bloatie."

"He was gross," Amy agreed. "Did he seem familiar to you?"

"Nope. Never saw the guy before in my life."

"How can you be so sure?"

Bill rolled his eyes. "When you've been in this business as long as I have you don't forget a face." He paused. "Even if it is all spongy from a week in the muddy Mississippi."

"Speaking of his face, I'm in the midst of trying to track him down. The medical examiner figures that he'd been dead, at the most, a week, at the least, three days. Could you help me get on the computer and show me where the missing persons databases are? Is it by state?"

"Can't, Ame. I'm off on patrol this morning. You'll figure it out. It's easy."

Amy didn't say anything. She was a better shot than Bill, but he was much more skilled on the computers.

Bill stood up to leave, then asked, "Hey, what happened with that guy that shot his wife?"

"I don't think they know yet. Took him off to the hospital and I guess he was breathing. Hopefully he's still alive."

"I heard that he hung himself with strips of the sheet. He must have been really desperate."

Amy gave Bill a slow look. "I think that attempting any form of suicide indicates a high level of desperation."

Bill stared at her. "You sound just like her."

"Like who?"

"Claire." Bill tapped her on the nose with his pointer finger. "Scary. That's the way she talks. Are you starting to be a Claire clone?"

Amy decided to break her rule of not touching him and picked up the report she had been going over and batted him with it.

After he ducked away from her swing, he asked, "Any chance you'll feel like a pizza tonight?" he asked.

"Only if it comes with mushrooms."

"Half of it can," Bill said.

"So just tell me this, to find out if someone's been reported missing, do I just go into the Wisconsin Public Records?"

"Depends on if they're missing from Wisconsin."

"I know. He's just as likely to be a Minnesota guy. I'll start on our side of the river, but plan to branch out later."

"If it's happened as recently as the medical examiner thinks, he might not be in the database yet. In fact, he probably won't be. He might not even have been reported as missing yet."

Amy stood up. "Okay, enough encouragement. Point me at the computer."

Bill put his large hand on her shoulder and pushed her toward the door of the computer room.

Amy said hi to another deputy who was scrolling through a database of numbers and sat down in front of one of the free computers. A psychedelic pattern of blending and swirling colors mesmerized her. She watched the twirling colors for a few moments, then managed to find her way into the Wisconsin Missing Persons database.

Working the database wasn't as hard as she had feared. She entered the data that she knew about their bloated man: red hair, blue eyes, 6 feet tall—probably around 200 pounds, but hard to tell because of the water gain—a small scar on his lower back that the coroner had called her about, and a tattoo on his left shoulder.

At first, she held off on the tattoo, just in case it wasn't mentioned. She was hoping the tattoo would make all the difference. Could there be that many men out there sporting a tree tattoo?

Age parameters: Dr. Davis said he was probably between thirty-five and forty-five. She had looked at his teeth as she said that. Just like with horses, Amy had thought, looking for the wear pattern. Then there was the dental work. To be on the safe side, Amy entered 30 < >50, even though that was a pretty large range.

She was counting on the tree tattoo to help winnow down the possibilities.

Two hits. A forty-eight-year-old pharmaceutical rep from Green Bay, way on the other side of the state. Didn't seem likely. The other was a thirty-one-year-old homeless vagrant. Again, the healthy, strong man that Amy had seen on the medical examiner's table didn't look like he had been missing any meals lately.

She started scrolling through the other recent missing persons and noted how most of them were under thirty and female: a nineteen-year-old girl, scholarship student at UW-Green Bay, pregnant, missing for five years; a twenty-eight-year-old woman who had diabetes that could render her unconscious; a fifty-year-old woman named Bethany, whose husband had been beating her, he had since been hit by a car; a twenty-one-year-old girl who had left a bowling alley after closing, made a phone call at two-thirty in the morning and was never seen again.

Amy pulled herself away from the computer screen. It was addictive, this dipping into all these strangers' lives, wondering where they might be, if they were even still alive. Some of them, she got a very strong feeling, had probably not survived the night of their disappearance. For all of them the end of the story might never be written. How horrible for the families.

It made her all the more determined to track down their John Doe. Even though his end was awful, at least his family would know what happened, could bury him, weep over him and lay him, and all their worries, to rest. Hopefully finding out who he was would help them figure out who his killer had been.

She found Claire at her desk, staring at some report but not really reading it, her eyes unfocused, her hand tapping an odd, nervous rhythm.

"Hey, Claire," Amy said quietly, not wanting to startle her.

Claire looked up with a ready smile, but Amy was surprised to see how tired she looked. The skin around her eyes looked bruised. She was wearing no make-up, not that she ever wore a lot. For the first time since Amy had worked with her, Claire looked vulnerable and raw.

"They say he's going to live," Claire told her.

Amy knew she was talking about Chet Baldwin.

"Glad to hear it. That's good news."

Claire shook her head. "You don't really know Chet, do you? I hope you're right—that it's good news. It's always hard to know when someone wants to die what kind of favor you're doing them by bringing them back."

Amy didn't know what to say. She hadn't really thought about suicide that much. She just knew what her job was.

"I just wanted to tell you how it's going with our John Doe. I checked the Wisconsin Missing Persons database and didn't see anyone who resembled our guy. But if the medical examiner's right about the date of death, he might not even be reported missing yet."

"You know, Amy, I want you to run with this one. You've been working with me for a couple years now and I think you're ready to take this one on. I'll be here if you need me, but I need to focus on this case."

"Really?" Amy felt pleasure and fear shoot through her system, kind of like the way she felt about skydiving, which she'd never done but thought about doing. "You think I'm ready?"

"Only one way to find out."

"Can I ask you one more question? What if this guy's from Minnesota? Is he still considered in our jurisdiction?"

Claire gave her a half smile. "Depends on where he died."

CHAPTER 6

Claire walked down the hallway, hearing the hollowness of her own footsteps, and smelling the ammonia in the air, the constant scent of hospitals. She wasn't one of those people who hated hospitals. She found them rather calming and reassuring, maybe because of a pleasant stay she had spent recovering from pneumonia when she was twelve. While being provided with all the chocolate milk she could drink, she read ten books in four days and thought she was in heaven.

She peeked into Chet's room and saw him asleep in the all-white bed, his head turned toward the window, his mouth ajar. His body was sprawled on the bed as if he'd been tossed there. Even from across the room she could see the ligature marks on his neck.

Earlier that morning a doctor had called and said Chet would survive the suicide attempt, but they weren't sure in what shape he would be, slight possibility of brain damage, a good chance of serious trauma to his esophagus.

Sympathy for him flooded Claire, but she pushed that feeling away. Unfortunately it was followed by guilt. She should have kept a closer eye on him. Her relationship with Chet had always been a little problematic. Rich so admired him—the good farmer, the great hunter, the county official. Claire had always felt like he was a bit of a bragger and also a bit corny.

While she could tell that Chet adored Anne, he did it in such a sappy way that she found it slightly offensive. Which strengthened her sense that he might have killed her. With Chet, Claire had always thought that he was pretty controlling and if Anne had done something wrong, he might have gone off on her. Claire had certainly never thought that Chet would try to kill himself, because of how highly he thought of himself. That was her mistake.

She hadn't officially put him on a suicide watch, which would have involved a more constant surveillance, instead of the hourly checking by the guards. On some level she had to admit she had failed Chet. What was she going to tell Rich?

Claire needed more information on Chet's current status, especially on the possible brain trauma. She walked over to the nurse's station and looked up at the board: Chet's nurse was Jennifer. A dark-haired woman at the desk was filling out reports and didn't even look up when Claire cleared her throat.

"Excuse me. Are you Jennifer?" Claire asked.

"I think she's back in the break room." The woman pointed to a small room behind the desk, still without looking up.

Peeking into the room Claire saw a young tow-headed woman sipping a cup of coffee and leaning against the counter. Claire asked if she was Jennifer. At the sight of Claire's uniform, the young woman pushed herself up as if she had been caught at something, said she was Jennifer, and asked how she could help.

"I'm here about Chet Baldwin. Can you give me an update on his prognosis?" As Claire heard herself using the lingo, she wondered if she had been watching too many medical shows on TV.

"Pretty good considering. You're the first person to check on him, poor guy. Are you related to him?" the girl asked.

"Haven't you been told about him?"

Jennifer gave her a quizzical look. "No, I came on an hour ago. Betty rushed out of here to do something and didn't tell me much, just his status. But I did read over the doctor's notes."

"No, I'm not related to him. His wife—" here Claire stopped, thinking about the scene in their house last night. "She's recently deceased. I'm not sure who else he has in his family. I know they had no children."

Jennifer held up her cup. "Coffee?"

Claire said, "That'd be great. Long night last night."

"I hear you. I'm working a double shift, came over from another floor." Jennifer poured her a cup and Claire took it gratefully.

"Dr. Ramstad thinks he's going to be okay. But he did a number on his larynx and he's going to have a very sore throat. I think they want to do an endoscopy on him later this afternoon, just to be sure there's no permanent damage. When I first got here, he was awake for a while, quiet but coherent—knew his name, knew what day it was, expressed his contempt of our current president—but he's been sleeping the last hour. So doesn't look like he has any significant brain damage. Exactly what happened to him?"

"He attempted suicide. You know that, right?"

"Yeah, Betty told me that. And there was some mention of it in his chart. Is he dangerous?"

"I think only to himself. But please keep a close eye on him. When will he be released?"

"Right now he's sedated. Dr. Ramstad wants to keep him in overnight. Just to watch him. I'm sure they'll want to do a psych evaluation. I suppose he might be able to leave tomorrow if they think he's stable enough."

"This gets rather tricky. We need to bring him in for questioning as soon as he's able." Claire gave the nurse her number. "I'll check back in later today, but I want to know when he's ready to leave."

"For sure. I'll make sure to pass on this information." The nurse looked toward his room. "He seems like a nice man."

Claire realized she had to be clearer with this nurse. "Why don't you call us when he becomes more lucid and we'll send over a man to stand guard outside his door. Just in case." Then she couldn't stop herself from saying the next words. "But he is a nice man."

● ● ●

"Then I threw up," Claire looked a little nauseous, just at the thought. "Over the side of the boat. I mean it was gross, this big bloated body stunk to high heavens and all, but still, I haven't thrown up in years."

Bridget watched her sister Claire. Even though she saw Claire often, every few days since moving to Fort St. Antoine, she suddenly noticed that her sister looked older: dark patches under her eyes, an actual sweep of gray growing up from her temple into her dark brown hair, and a hunching of her shoulders.

Claire had called Bridget at the pharmacy where she worked in Wabasha and asked if they could have lunch. They had met at the Sunshine Diner and were halfway through their bowls of chili.

Claire continued, "So I'm worried. I mean, I haven't had my period in nearly seven weeks, I threw up, I've turned into a bitch, I feel weird. What if I'm pregnant? Oh my god, Bridget, what would I do?"

"Calm down. Let me ask you a few questions. Are you sleeping okay?" Bridget asked.

"What's that got to do with anything? Not bad, but I'm doing this weird three o'clock in the morning—bong—wide awake routine. Can't go back to sleep. Toss and turn for an hour or two."

"How's your body thermostat these days?" Bridget continued her questions. "Hot? Sweaty?"

"Yeah, this weather seems to be really getting to me. Like right now, I'm drenched in sweat."

"Well, I know I don't need to tell you this, but you absolutely need to take a pregnancy test. However, what I'm thinking is it might be menopause."

Claire wiped her hand across her face as if she could wipe this possibility away. "You think? It crossed my mind, but I'm only forty-five. Mom didn't go into menopause until her mid fifties."

"Yeah, but she had two kids and a miscarriage. That can push it back. And everyone is different."

"God, menopause." A smile broke across Claire's face and she looked younger. "That would be great. And it would explain everything. I can't tell you what a relief that would be."

"Well, first take a pregnancy test just to be sure. Then get your butt to your gynecologist and get checked out. Slight chance it could be a thyroid problem and that's completely treatable. They can test your hormone level and you'll know for sure what's going on." Even though Bridget knew Claire would not want to hear it, she couldn't help adding, "You do look tired."

"It's been a crappy couple days. First the stinky bloated body, then Chet and everything I told you. You can imagine. And Rich and I aren't getting along."

"How long have you two been together now?"

"About seven years."

"The magic number. That's when Chuck and I split up. But that doesn't mean you and Rich will … have problems." Bridget thought back to her marriage. She saw Chuck every once in a while. He had remarried, a woman who liked cars and beer more than she had. She had to give him credit for being a good father to Rachel. He came and got her at least twice a week and now that she was older, he even kept her overnight sometimes.

"Don't say that. It's just that Rich thinks he can go barging into my business, telling me what to do …"

"Big sister," Bridget shook her head. "You've always had to be right about everything. Maybe it's time you learned to listen."

"How can you say that?" Claire's voice rose above the clanking sounds of the coffee shop.

"Because it's true. And I'm telling you to take a pregnancy test. Come back to the pharmacy with me."

• • •

As little as he wanted to go back to Chet's farm, Rich knew he had to check on all the animals. Let the horses out to pasture. Feed the dog. Bentley had been Anne's pride and joy, some kind of Australian herding dog. He wasn't even sure it was really a breed, but the dog was smart as a whip. Almost pure black, it was a fierce fighter, which made it an excellent dog for watching over the barnyard.

After pulling into the driveway, Rich went right to the barn. No reason to go into the house, plus Claire'd probably have his hide if he befouled her crime scene any more than he already had.

Rich pushed open the door of Chet's barn. Not sure where the light was, he started to walk across to the horse stalls, when a very low, very deep growl crawled across the floor and rode up his body.

"Bentley?" Rich said, not sure where the sound was coming from. "Is that you, buddy?"

The barn was dark and the dog, as he remembered it, was darker. Rich's eyes were not yet accustomed to the gloom and he found himself standing in the middle of a mound of hay, turning slowly around, trying to locate the dog before it made any kind of nasty move.

The chainsaw growl stopped.

Rich waited, sucking in a lungful of damp air perfumed with horse manure and field clippings.

He took a step toward the first horse stall and the growl started up, louder than ever. The hair on the back of his hands felt tight, his jaw seized up on him like an old wrench that needed oil. There was something about that sound that grabbed him in the guts and yanked.

Rich reminded himself he knew how to work with animals—talk to them, don't let them know you're afraid—but it might be too late for that. "Hey, buddy, hey, boy, are you hungry?"

Use his name, with a little sharper tone, commanding, not pleading. "Bentley, come."

The dog's growl rasped up a notch higher.

Just when Rich was thinking of backing out of the barn he saw Bentley. The dog was between him and the door, fear raising his long black fur on his back, his teeth shining in his huge muzzle.

Rich checked his pockets, nothing. He was hoping he might find an old energy bar, something he could bribe the dog with.

Looking around the barn, he tried to find something he might use against Bentley, not to hurt him, more just to fend him off. He saw a broom leaning in a corner and decided that was the ticket. In the slowest motion he could manage, Rich backed up and put his hand on the broom and slowly brought it around to protect his front.

Bentley was on ready alert, too close to the door for Rich to try to get by him. With broom in hand, he knew he could do what he needed to do.

Incrementally inching around, Rich turned his back on Bentley and leaned on the broom as if he had absolutely nothing on his mind. He relaxed his shoulders, slouched comfortably on the broom handle and hummed a quiet song.

The growling stopped.

Rich kept up his charade of unconcerned farmer, completely ignoring the dark beast by the door.

Bentley unhackled.

Rich could see the dog out of the corner of his eye. Easing his weight down on the broom handle, he gently went down on his haunches to the floor, still humming.

Bentley took a step towards Rich. Then he lifted his head and sniffed.

As easily as he could Rich held out a hand in Bentley's direction.

Bentley took another step, lowering his head as he came.

A few steps later and Bentley was sniffing Rich's hand. After another few moments, Rich set the broom down, turned his hand up and rubbed the underside of Bentley's jaw. The beast leaned into his hand.

"You hungry, boy?" Rich said in a low, clear voice.

The tail thumped.

Raising himself up while continuing to pet the dog, Rich stayed relaxed. He was pretty sure Bentley was won over, but didn't want to startle him "Let's go get something to eat, Bentley."

At the word, "eat," the dog's big dark ears pricked up.

"Eat, Bentley," Rich said, and slapped his other hand against his pant leg.

The dog moved in closer and wagged his tail harder.

"Where's your food?" Rich asked and the dog barked an answer.

Chet had told him it was in the big galvanized steel garbage can, mouse-proofed. Rich saw the can in the corner of the barn and the empty bowl next to it. There was a light switch right behind the can on a support beam.

As he took a step toward the can, Bentley swirled around him in happiness, a different dog.

Still being cautious to make no sudden moves, Rich turned on the light. He slowly lifted the top off the garbage can, found an old measuring cup half buried in the chow and filled the bowl with food.

Bentley dove into it when Rich set the bowl on the barn floor.

Hopefully, he wouldn't need to feed him again. Hopefully, Chet would be home before evening.

CHAPTER 7

The Army Corps of Engineers maps were spread out all over the conference table. Amy was staring at them as if she could see the way the current would flow, the speed of the water, the underwater sandbars, and low-ebb pools that would influence how a body might move downstream. In fact, all she really hoped to see were the places where someone could easily dump a body.

What the medical examiner had told her was that the body could have been in the water anywhere from three to seven days. What the man from the AC of E told her was that a piece of wood would drift down the river at a speed of three miles a day. But the problem was that this body had been tied to some kind of weight and they had no way of knowing how long it had stayed tethered: In other words, the body might have been in the water for seven days, but only floating free for two.

Amy guessed that the body had been dumped in Lake Pepin and probably not further up the river. Looking back upstream to the curves of the Mississippi and the St. Croix rivers as they flowed into Lake Pepin, she just didn't see any way that a body wouldn't get caught up on something before it entered the relatively open and free-flowing body of the lake.

As Amy perused the series of charts that showed the lake, the mid-channel sailing line, various buoys and landings, she noticed that the top of Lake Pepin was at mile-marker 786 and it ended at 765. The guide said that the mile-markers were measured from the Ohio River northward. An odd way to do it, she thought. She would have numbered from the source up by Lake Itasca, but she wasn't an engineer.

So the lake was twenty-one miles long just as she had always been told. The Point No Point buoy was about at mile-marker 779, so that meant there were only seven miles above it where the body might have been dumped.

But it hadn't really been dumped. It had been deposited relatively carefully. Probably using a boat. How else would they get it out far enough to make sure it wouldn't show up if the water level sank? That meant that the body could have been carried by boat really from any place on the river. Certainly didn't narrow things down. Amy looked up at the dotted acoustic-tile ceiling in the conference room, not sure that the maps were helping at all.

Just then Jeremy walked in. "Finding any good clues on the ceiling?"

Amy was very happy when Jeremy had joined the sheriff's department a few months ago. His arrival made her no longer the youngest or newest kid on the block. Tall and lanky, wide-apart blue eyes with a sprinkle of blackheads along the lines of his nose, Jeremy looked like he was sixteen and not quite grown into his body, but he claimed to be all of twenty.

Only twenty-three herself, Amy wanted to separate herself from him so the two of them weren't lumped together as the youngsters. She had mixed feelings about showing him the ropes.

"You heard about our floater?"

Jeremy nodded, then said, "I heard Bill found it."

"With Claire," Amy corrected, then continued. "Whatever. I'm trying to figure out where it might have gone in the water."

His face lit up as he thought about what she had told him. "You mean, where it was dumped?"

"Well, that's what I was just wondering. I wouldn't say it was really dumped. That makes the action sound careless. Whoever put it in the river, and you'd think it would have to be more than one person because that guy was heavy, didn't want it found. They tied something to his ankle, like a concrete block or a stone. Something heavy. So they probably used a boat to get it out into deeper water."

"It was found by Maiden Rock?"

"Yes, just south of the park. I'm wondering if it's worth taking a look around at that wooden pier in the park and asking around the town. You never know what people see sometimes."

"That sounds smart."

"Yeah, the more I think about it, the more convinced I am that the body was put into the water quite close to where it was found."

"How so?"

"Well, it was discovered late afternoon by some fishermen. You didn't see the body, but by the time it was found it was bloated into a big and white object, like a buoy. Fairly easy to spot from a distance away. It's hard for me to imagine that it could float down the river for very long, especially on a high-traffic day like yesterday, without someone seeing it."

"Is this, like, your case?"

"It doesn't really work that way around here, Jeremy. We're a team. Claire's the head investigator, but we all help out. Everyone except her has a rotation and we do what we can while we're on duty."

"You going to check it out?"

Amy wondered what she might find down at the Maiden Rock Park. You just never knew what someone might have left lying around as they struggled to get a body into a boat.

•   •   •

Meg watched Curt walk up the driveway with her usual excitement, and an odd longing—or maybe it was yearning—that hit her below the belly button. They had decided he should park in town and walk the six blocks to Rich's house. They weren't taking any chances; they didn't want anyone to notice his car. That way if Claire or Rich came home early, he could slip out her bedroom window, climb down the oak tree that rubbed against the house, and disappear into the woods behind the farm, circling around until he got back to his car. No adult the wiser.

Claire and Rich had been pretty clear with her. No boys in the house when they were gone. But where were she and Curt supposed to hang out? At the grocery store in Pepin? The library, and get shushed by the librarian who knew them and watched them like a kindly hawk? Certainly not at school. They sometimes sat at the coffee shop, but that got expensive, and after an hour or so, they started to get dirty looks from the owner.

They could always head for the backcountry, and often they did, but parking on farm roads got a little old too. Once Mr. Swenson blocked them in with his tractor. They hadn't noticed him at first, too busy seeing how long they could kiss without breathing, and then there he was at the window, asking them what they were doing. A rhetorical question, but for some reason one that Curt felt obliged to try to answer. "A kind of contest," he started while Meg pinched his underarm to quiet him. She had smiled and said, "We got lost." Keep it simple. She had learned this lesson from her mom, who told her that one of the mistakes criminals frequently make was they complicated matters and got caught in their own lies.

Meg ran down the stairs and let Curt in, even though the door wasn't locked and he could have let himself in.

"Something to drink?" she asked. It was another beastly hot day. All she was wearing was a tank top and the shortest shorts she owned. In this kind of humid weather, she didn't like the feel of anything on her skin.

Curt was wearing a holey t-shirt and baggy jeans. He held up his hand as if waiting to have something placed in it. "I'll have a martini."

"Right. Like you could even drink one if I made it for you."

"Right. Like you could even make one."

"We've got the bartending book. But I'm not sure we have all the ingredients." Meg laughed, imagined the two of them drinking martinis together. She had had a sip of one once. The drink had tasted like gasoline.

Curt put his palm on her back, right between her shoulder blades. She loved him touching her. He didn't do it much in public, which made it that more special when he reached out and put a hand on her in a quiet moment, especially when they weren't just all over each other.

"A big glass of water would be fine," he said.

"With ice?"

"Yes, please and a slice of lemon if you've got it." He had pushed his voice up into a falsetto, pretending he was a socialite of some sort.

One thing Meg had noticed about Curt was that when he was nervous, he started to play act he was someone else. She found it hysterical, but also saw that it was his way of keeping himself at a distance. Sometimes she played along, sometimes she just let him go off on his own.

"Coming right up." But before she could step into the kitchen he had slid his hand down her spine and pulled her close to him.

They kissed and she could taste the sweetness of toothpaste on his tongue and salt on his lips: an interesting combination, like a Salted Nut Roll.

"How far are we going to go today?" he asked.

"Just to the brink."

●   ●   ●

Once she got back to the sheriff's department from lunch with the pregnancy test in her purse, Claire could think of nothing else. It was going to be a long afternoon if she had to wait until she got home to take it. Also, she hadn't called Rich yet about Chet. She so hated to tell him what had happened to his good friend. She was afraid that he would blame her and, worse, she was afraid, that in this instance, he might be absolutely right.

Claire was trying to learn to not put things off. Otherwise they just became this huge glob of worry and weight on her shoulders and she walked around feeling them pressing her down all day long.

So she decided to get at least one thing over with and held the pregnancy test next to her uniform. First, she went to the bathroom and locked the door. Impatient as she was when she tore the package open, she forced herself to read all the directions. Lord knows she didn't want to do anything wrong and get a false reading. Just as she was about to sit down on the toilet, someone knocked on the door.

"Someone's in here," Claire said and then realized how stupid that sounded. "It's me, Claire. I'll be out in a minute."

She pulled out the dipstick or whatever it was called and as quickly as possible did the required maneuvers, letting a full stream hit the white stick.

She didn't want whichever woman was standing outside the door to see what she was doing. But there sat the box and she didn't want to shove the wet stick into her pocket—that might ruin the process. First she stuffed the box into the bottom of the wastebasket, then washed her hands and put several wet paper towels over it to completely cover it. She was still left with the moist stick. She carefully covered it with another paper towel and opened the door, acting as though she was still drying her hands.

Crystal, the new secretary, was waiting outside. "Hey, Claire, how's it going today? Hot as all get out, huh?"

Just what she didn't need. A conversation about the weather. "Yeah, sure is. It's all yours," she said and walked away.

When Claire sat down at her desk, still carefully holding the paper towel, she saw the sheriff headed her way. Muttering swear words under her breath, she pulled open her top drawer and put the paper towel and the stick inside.

"Claire, how'd it go at the hospital?" the sheriff asked.

For the oddest moment, she thought he was asking her about the results of her pregnancy test. She shook her head as if to chase those thoughts away and launched into her report about Chet. "They said they'd call as soon as they did an evaluation. I didn't get to talk to him—he was sleeping and I didn't want to wake him—but the nurse said he's pretty with it."

"No chance of him trying something again, in the hospital, is there?"

"I don't think so. I made it clear that he needed to be watched. They've got him sedated and his room is right across the hall from the nurses' station. So they're keeping a pretty good eye on him. After the tests, sounds like they might even let him go tomorrow."

"That'd be good. We need to talk to him. I think we should line up a psychiatrist to have on hand for that conversation. We need to do everything right this time."

Claire could hear him trying not to blame her for what happened to Chet. "Yes, sir. We will."

Her phone rang and the sheriff walked off as she answered it. "Watkins."

"Hey," Rich said.

For a moment, Claire thought of opening the drawer and reading the information on the stick while she was talking to him. Then she knew that might not be a good idea. One piece of bad news at a time. But would a pregnancy be bad news for Rich? He had said that Meg was enough kid for him, but she had always wondered.

"How's your day?" she asked, stalling.

"Not too bad. I went over to Chet's and fed the dog. Bentley wasn't too friendly but we managed to work it out."

"Bentley?"

"The dog. How's Chet?"

"Well, I've been meaning to call you. Pretty busy here today. Chet—" Claire didn't know how to tell Rich that Chet had tried to kill himself. She didn't want to say it. She'd gloss over it and explain it more completely when she got home that night. "Chet didn't do so well last night. He freaked out. Just too much for him. So he's in the hospital now, under sedation."

"Geez, really? I'm kinda surprised. Not that he wouldn't be really upset by what happened, but he's always weathered difficulties pretty well. Should I stop down to see him?"

"Oh, no. I don't think that would be good. They're going to have a psychiatrist talk to him, evaluate him. I think they've got him pretty doped up right now. He's probably too groggy to talk."

"What have you found out?"

"About what?"

"You know. About what happened at his house last night. I know you were going to run some tests on the guns and all. I've lived with you for enough years that I know what some of the procedure is now."

Claire felt a laugh push up her throat, but stifled it. "Nothing conclusive. They both have traces of residue on their hands, but then we know that Chet held the gun. You saw it in his hands—so that doesn't really prove anything"

"Sorry about last night, er, this morning I guess."

Rich was always better at apologizing than she was, but she could at least echo him. "Me too."

"What time will I see you?"

"I won't be too late. I'm wiped out. Not much sleep last night."

After they hung up, Claire sat and stared at the drawer. She knew the test was finished. In under a minute, in the privacy of your own work bathroom, you could find out if your life was going to change beyond recognition.

She didn't know what she would do if she was pregnant, but she couldn't see having a baby at her age. She had a feeling Meg would be fine with it. Her daughter might even think it was funny, exciting and possibly a little ridiculous. That's what Claire would think about it if it were happening to another woman her own age. She had heard of women in their mid-forties having children, but she couldn't imagine retiring and still having a kid at home.

Her guess was that Rich would be pleased if she found out she was pregnant. He had been a good father to Meg, even though she was not his own child. He liked all the parts of being a couple better than Claire did: the joint checking account, the deciding what car they needed next, the divvying up of the chores, even the compromises. Especially the compromises. He did all that stuff better than she did.

She could just see his face looking down on his own progeny with pride. He'd probably be better at changing diapers than she was. At least breast-feeding would be out of his scope.

She pulled the drawer open and yanked the paper towel off the stick.

A negative sign.

It was negative and her heart sunk and then bobbed back up again. No baby blues.

Not pregnant, which meant she was starting to slip and slide into menopause. No babies ever again. Looked like that part of her life was truly over.

CHAPTER 8

W ant to go swimming?" Amy teased Bill as they drove across
the railroad tracks in Maiden Rock and headed down to
the park and the beach. She knew how much he hated the water.
He didn't even own a swim suit. She herself needed to lose about
twenty pounds before she'd look decent in a suit so maybe it was
good he didn't like to swim.

Bill squinted his eyes in what she liked to call his safari look.
"I did my one swim for the summer. Plus, the water is turning
that weird shade of green it gets in later summer."

"Some kind of harmless algae," Amy reassured him.

"I'm not going in. No way," Bill said.

"Not even if we see something out in the water, say just ten
feet or so off the dock? You wouldn't jump in and retrieve that?"

"No, but I'd hold your clothes for you so you could do it.
I'd be there to pull you back out of the water."

"What a guy." He slowly drove the squad car closer to the
dock. "Why don't you stop here? Who knows, there might be
tire prints or something. Wouldn't want to mess them up."

"I think you've been watching too much TV. Doesn't happen like that in real life. Besides, we don't even know if this is
where they put the body into the water."

"It's my very educated guess. As someone famous says in a much fancier way, the simplest solution is most often right. I'm hoping that whoever dumped our John Doe's body was A, in a hurry, B, drunk, C, careless and D, assuming it would never be found. If any or all of those factors are true, we might find something."

Bill looked over at her with an impressed expression on his face. "You're so organized. I bet you were good at school. You should have been a school teacher, not a cop."

Amy thought back to her two years at a junior college before she went into the police academy. "I thought about it, but cops make more money and get to retire earlier. Plus I figured I'd get to meet more guys."

"Now the truth comes out."

She giggled as she stepped out of the squad car.

They both looked out toward the dock and the water. There had been no rain for over a week so Amy didn't really expect to see any tire prints. Slowly they walked toward the dock, searching the ground. The few tire marks that were clear looked like they had been made by bikes. Amy saw twist-off tops, cigarette butts, and a gum wrapper, but nothing that looked out of place. When they got to the dock, they took a few steps down it, peering into the water on either side.

"I'm guessing he worked with his hands, our bloated floater," Bill said. "He was a big guy. Construction. Maybe a farmer, but I doubt it. Otherwise he'd be known around here."

"The medical examiner did say his hands were well callused. So good guess."

"Hey, not a guess. I can play Sherlock Holmes too, noticing the odd detail, figuring out the occupation of said dead body. Just put a big hat on me and stuff a pipe in my mouth and I'll tell you what's what."

"I'd rather not." Amy laughed. "I can see construction being a possibility. He did something that caused him to get cut up from time to time. The ME showed me a couple deep cuts on his hands that had healed over. So whatever he did, he'd been at it for a while."

"Weird that he was naked." Bill scuffed his shoe on the wooden slats of the dock.

"Maybe he was naked when he was killed."

"What, like he got caught in the act?"

"Can't rule anything out yet. But I guess I figure that whoever dumped him just didn't want us to be able to figure anything out from his clothes."

"At least they didn't cut his fingers off."

"Well, that's for sure." Amy walked to the end of the dock. Stretching out into the water about forty feet, it was a removable dock that was taken out of the water in late fall and stored someplace. Boats were not permanently moored there, but visitors to the town often tied up to the dock for the day. Fishermen would tie up and wander up to Ole's for a brew. She checked the wooden planks carefully although she didn't expect to find anything. The wind and people's feet would have knocked any evidence into the water.

When they reached the end of the dock, Bill grabbed her and acted as if he was going to push her in.

"Don't you dare." She squirmed in his strong hands.

"I'm your superior officer. If I say jump, you have to jump." He held her close to the side of the dock.

"Only if there's a good reason."

"I'd come up with one mighty quick." He leaned down and kissed the back of her neck, then let her go.

She had asked Bill to not be intimate with her during work hours so she forced herself to ignore his kiss. "Did you bring the binoculars?"

"In the car. Along with my polarized sunglasses," he said. "As my sub-ordinate, I think you better run and get them."

"Okay, but don't find anything without me."

"I'll wait." He sat down at the end of the dock and took his shoes off.

When Amy came back with the binoculars and glasses, Bill was dangling his very white feet in the water. She stood above him, scanning the shallow bay that formed in the curve of Maiden Rock. While the binoculars cut the glare on the water, they could do nothing about the green algae that was crowding into the area.

She wished she could tell how the water circulated in the harbor. "What if we got a small buoy, put it in the water about twenty or thirty feet out and watched which way it floated? That might give us some idea of the current here and we could extrapolate backwards and find the weight he was tied to."

Bill laughed. "Great idea, but I doubt it would work. Too many factors. I'd say we look around the shore a little more, then head back to Durand. I think our little field trip is going to be a bust, Amster."

"Do you think there's any chance that the sheriff could be persuaded to dredge the bottom of the bay?"

"No and no," Bill said as they stepped off the dock. "First, he wouldn't. Secondly, so what if we found the cement block or whatever, what does it prove? We still got nothing."

Amy pulled away from him. He was right and she knew it. One of her fantasies about being a deputy was that she would find just the right thing at the right moment to put the whole case together. She kicked at the sand and still all she saw was dirt. Which is what you should find on a beach in Wisconsin. Maybe an agate if you're lucky.

She walked over to the big green dumpster. Just on the odd chance there might be something of interest, she went on tip-toe and looked in. A slight squeal slipped out of her mouth when she caught a flash of red.

"Bill, come here. I think I found something."

•   •   •

When Rich got home he was happy to find Meg stretched out on the deck of the house in the shade with a book, wearing a bathing suit and listening to his old transistor radio.

"You're actually using that antique?" he asked.

"Seems to fit my mood. Some songs sound better on it." She smiled up at him, then wrinkled her nose. "Hey, what was up with you and Mom last night?"

He realized he hadn't told Meg what had happened to Chet. Somehow he felt like he could manage it now. He didn't feel so completely thrown. Maybe it was not coming out of sleep, maybe it was even half a day's time, but it might have been his successful confrontation with Bentley. He felt more able to take on what the world dished him.

"Chet's wife was killed last night."

Meg sat up, the book falling onto the deck. "You're kidding. How did that happen?"

"She was shot."

"Who did it?"

"Not sure yet. She might have done it to herself."

"You mean like suicide."

"Yup."

"Doesn't seem like her. I mean I didn't know her very well or anything, but she always was so upbeat."

Rich didn't want to go into it with her anymore, so he asked a question that she never got tired of answering. "Where's your boyfriend today?"

Meg glanced up into the woods. "Oh, I think he's taking a hike. We might get together later, but he's got to help his dad with the haying this afternoon."

"He's a good kid."

"Rich, he's not a kid. He's going to be eighteen in two months."

"Old enough to join the army and get married."

"Neither of which he'll do, I'm sure."

"I'm glad to hear that."

•   •   •

"I want to see her." The woman's voice was blunt.

The secretary had told Claire that the gravel-gray haired woman looking over the counter at Claire was Anne Baldwin's sister. Looking at her more closely, Claire figured her older sister. Claire hoped so, because the woman looked a lot older than Anne had been.

Claire guessed that the woman was in her fifties, which meant she had a good fifteen years on Anne. But then she also looked as if she had lived those years in a hard way, deep lines around her mouth from smoking, drooping eyes from drinking. But she wore a clean white shirt and jeans, and when she put her hands on the counter to plead her case, her long nails sported red polish.

But there was a resemblance. Where Anne's hair was short and blond, the sister's hair was peppered gray, but they had the same wide mouth and light blue eyes. This woman was an older, tougher version.

"There's just me and my sister left around here. Our parents are gone. Brothers moved away. She's all I had left," the woman said in explanation of her request. At this point the woman's voice trembled and she bowed her head and said, "I know you need someone to identify her."

"That really won't be necessary, Ms...."

"Colette Burns. That was Anne's maiden name too."

Claire continued, "She's already been identified by her husband."

"Good enough, but I need to see her. I want to see my sister." Colette hesitated for a moment, then added, "Please. I think it's the only way I'll really believe that she's dead."

It was unusual to get such a request and when it happened, Claire tried to discourage the relatives from this kind of viewing, asking them to wait until after the funeral home had done their work on the body. Usually the families agreed to this. But Colette seemed particularly persistent. And there was something about the woman that touched Claire—probably her situation. Claire could easily see herself asking the same thing if anything happened to Bridget. Plus, it would be a good opportunity to talk to the woman, see what Colette could tell her about Anne's mental state.

"She's at the morgue in the hospital. Just a couple blocks away. I'll take you over there."

In the squad car, Claire asked Colette how she had found out about her sister.

"Somebody told me. They must have heard it on the news. I tried to call the house and got no one so I called you guys."

"I'm sorry we didn't get in touch with you. We didn't realize she had any family close by."

Colette said, "I'm not too close. Live over west a ways. You know Waseca? It's in Minnesota."

"Yes," Claire said. "I'm from Minnesota originally. Is that where you two grew up? Waseca?"

"Close to there. Out in the country."

"Makes sense to me that Anne grew up on a farm. She was always so good with animals, especially that dog of hers."

There was a stunned silence, then Colette said, "I gave her Bentley. Did you know my sister?"

"Oh, I'm sorry I didn't mention that. The man I live with, Rich Haggard, is good friends with her husband Chet."

"Where is Chet? I tried him at the house a bunch of times. Is he okay? And what happened to her? I couldn't quite take it all in. All I heard was that it was some kind of shooting."

"Yes. We're not sure of much more." Claire debated for a moment, then decided she might as well tell Colette what she knew. "Late last night Chet called and asked for help. When I arrived on the scene, your sister was already dead from a gunshot wound. Chet was in a state of shock. I have to tell you that there is the slight chance that Anne killed herself, but we're really not sure yet of anything."

"Anne has been low lately, but I can't see her doing something like that. Not in her nature. But I'd be surprised if it's Chet. If you knew them at all you know that he doted on her."

They pulled into the parking lot of the hospital. Claire asked her, "Why do you say that Anne wasn't doing so well recently?"

"She's been hinting that they've had problems. She never told me exactly what was going on, but she did let on that something was wrong. I asked her to come stay with me for a while, but she said she couldn't leave Chet. Not really like her. If only..." Colette stopped and started to shake, sucking back tears.

Claire reached out and touched her arm while Colette calmed herself.

Colette rubbed a hand through her hair and wiped her eyes. "Sorry about that. I'm really not much of a crier, but I just can't believe she's gone. It's like it shoots through me. I forget for a moment, then—blam—I get hit with it again. Anne's dead. My little sister's dead."

Hearing Colette say the phrase, "my little sister," Claire's mind flew right to Bridget and how she would react if anything happened to her own little sister. A stabbing sorrow hit her too.

"I can't imagine how you're feeling," Claire said, trying to regain her composure. "It has to be a nightmare."

"I just can't believe it."

Claire got out of the car quickly so Colette wouldn't see her wiping tears from her own eyes. When Colette stood on the sidewalk, still crying, Claire slipped an arm under hers and led her into the hospital. They walked down a long hallway and took the elevator down a floor to the morgue.

Holding onto Colette's arm felt like the least she could do to comfort the woman. Sometimes just having someone touch you was all that was needed when the going got rough.

Claire sat Colette down, went into the morgue and arranged to have the gurney wheeled into a private room. A few minutes later, they were standing over the covered gurney that held Anne Baldwin. Colette was holding a smashed Kleenex in her hand. She looked up at Claire and nodded her head.

Claire gently lifted the sheet off the woman's face, pulling it down to her shoulders. In death, Anne looked cold and tired, face just a shade warmer than the sheet. A lot of her energy had been in her eyes and they were shut. The round bullet hole in the middle of her forehead looked unreal, more like an ornament than a wound.

At this sight, Colette pulled her breath in and clamped her hands over her mouth.

"It's hard. I know," Claire said, surprised at how much it was affecting her to see her friend like this. It was as if she had forgotten who was under the sheet, who this dead woman was.

Colette shook her head with a jerk, then burst out, "Now I know for sure she didn't do it. No question."

Claire looked down at the white face of Anne more carefully. "Why do you say that?"

Colette's hand hovered over Anne's forehead, pointing down at the bruised hole in the middle. "Anne would never shoot herself in the face. She loved the way she looked. She took such good care of herself, her skin and all. She would never have shot herself there. In the heart, yes, but never the face."

CHAPTER 9

A crumpled piece of rusty-red fabric tucked into a cardboard box is what had caught her eye. Since the edge of the dumpster was over her head, Amy asked Bill to lift her up so she could reach down into the dumpster and see what it was. She didn't want to admit to him that she was hoping it was a blood-soaked rag or sheet.

"Gross. What's down there?" he asked.

"You are the most finicky cop I've ever known. I'm not sure, but I think what I'm seeing is something sort of reddish."

He bent over and cupped his hands together, offering her a boost. She stepped into his hands and was amazed, as always, at how easily he lifted her weight. Amy hung over the rounded metal side into the interior of the dumpster, trying not to breathe, and managed to hook a finger around an edge of the fabric. Once she got a firm grip on it, she put her weight back into Bill's hand-stirrup and let him lower her back down to the ground.

"What've you got there?"

"Let's see," Amy gently shook out the red fabric and saw the she was in fact holding a t-shirt. Not stained red, but obviously dyed a rusty-red. Amy held up the red t-shirt and they both looked it over. The garment was a very large and fairly dirty red t-shirt. When she scrutinized the label, she read 100 percent cotton and then XXL. The shirt was turned inside out so Amy couldn't tell yet if anything was printed on the front or back.

"Why would someone throw this perfectly good t-shirt in the dumpster?" Bill asked.

"I don't know. A million reasons. Didn't like it. Spilled something on it. But it's definitely our mystery man's size, extra extra large." Amy said. "There are no holes in it, but it does look like it's been worn and it's kinda dusty."

"What is that all over it?" Bill asked and ran his finger down the shirt.

Amy said, "You know I suppose we should be wearing gloves."

"Oh, come on. You can't leave fingerprints on fabric. What are we going to mess up? We're not even sure that it's connected to bloaty boy."

"I just have a feeling."

"Gosh, that is so girlie. You're such a smart cop, I forget you have that woman's intuition."

Amy ignored that remark, but slipped her gloves on and then rubbed a finger down the t-shirt fabric. She sniffed the light-colored powder that collected on her fingertip and then stared at it closely. "I think it's sawdust."

"Throw it back in the garbage. It's nothing."

"Let me turn it right side out first." Amy grabbed the bottom of the shirt and straightened it out. Nothing on the back. When she turned it around, her heart jumped in her chest. "Look."

"What?" Bill asked, staring at the shirt. "I don't see nothing."

"Anything," Amy couldn't help saying. "You don't see the tree?"

"So? What's with a tree?"

"Oh, maybe I didn't tell you—bloaty guy—he had this exact symbol of a tree tattooed on his shoulder. Which, I'm guessing, would make this his t-shirt."

"Great. Now we have a guy who we can't identify with a shirt that has no writing on it."

"But maybe it means something," Amy suggested. "Like it's the symbol of a business or an organization or something."

Bill turned the shirt around so he could see the tree symbol again. "Yeah. I think you're right. I got an idea. Feel like a beer?"

"We're not quite off duty, my dear."

"Let's go to Sven's anyways."

As they walked into Sven's Bar and Grill, Amy was hit by the smell of old cigarettes and stale beer. Funny how it seemed stronger in the middle of the day when the bar was nearly empty. No people-smell to tone it down.

"Well, if it isn't two fine officers of the law," Sven himself said. Sven, broad as a beam, could barely see over the bar. Amy figured he was no more than five feet tall. He sported a patchy dark beard and slicked his wispy brown hair back with some kind of gel. His gruff voice sounded like it came out of a well. She didn't know him well, but she knew he ran a tight ship. They didn't get very many calls from his establishment.

"What can I do you for? Set you up with two frosty ones?" Sven asked as they settled onto bar stools.

Bill looked at her and Amy said, "Thanks, but not at the moment."

"Show him the t-shirt," Bill told her.

Amy held up the shirt for Sven's perusal. They had stopped off at the squad car on the way to the bar and she had bagged it, folding it carefully so the tree symbol showed clearly through the plastic.

"The tree guy," Sven said.

Amy refrained from saying, "Duh."

Bill asked the obvious question. "What tree guy?"

Sven shook his head. "Not sure what his name is or anything. He's come in a couple times. He's a tree removal and trimmer guy. Don't think he's from around here, but I'm not sure. In fact, if I remember correctly, he's a Vikings fan."

"Only someone from Minnesota would have that kind of bad taste," Bill said. He was a hard-core Packers fan. "Interesting. Anything else you can tell us? He a regular? When was the last time you saw him in here?"

Sven combed his hands through his scant beard. "Within the last couple weeks, I'd say. Couldn't swear to it, though."

"Can you describe him?" Amy asked.

"Oh, you know, about yea-high," Sven held a hand out about a foot above his own head. "About yea-wide." He held his two short arms out as far as they would stretch. "And to hear him talk, about yea-long." He held his hand out as far as he could in front of the fly of his jeans.

"Into the ladies?" Bill asked.

"If you believed what he said."

"What color hair?" Amy asked.

Sven scratched his own thinning scalp. "Geez, you know, it's dark in here most of the time. I don't pay much attention to that sort of stuff."

"Could it be red?"

Sven shrugged. "Could be. Kinda dark red."

"Ever noticed any kind of tattoo?" Amy asked.

"Where?" Sven fired back.

Amy couldn't help laughing. "You know, your mind's in the gutter, Sven. On his shoulder."

"Not that I remember."

"Was he with anyone when he came in?"

"Not that I recall."

Amy felt like they had pushed Sven's memory about as far as it would stretch. "Thanks for help. If you remember anything else, give us a call."

"Yeah, thanks," Bill said as he was looking longingly at the tap on the edge of the bar.

"Can we get a six-pack to go?" Amy asked.

After Sven handed them the six-pack, Amy grabbed Bill's arm and pulled him toward the door. "So it sounds like he was down here for business, not pleasure, if he is our guy."

Bill shrugged. "Who knows, maybe both."

• • •

Claire decided she didn't want to take Colette back to the department. The woman needed to recover, and sugar was always good for shock so she took her to a little coffee shop in the basement of the hospital.

"They make good pie here," Claire advised her.

Colette reached out and took the first piece of pie that came to hand. Cherry, it looked like. Claire followed suit. There wasn't a fruit pie she didn't like. Both of them grabbed coffee. Claire paid for it. The least she could do.

Once they were sitting at a table and Colette had a few bites of pie inside her, Claire asked her an easy, non-threatening question. "How far is Waseca from here?"

"Well, depends on which way you come. You know, as the crow flies, it's only about sixty miles, but then there's the lake, you see. You have to get around the lake. Usually takes me about two hours to get home."

"Did you see Anne very often?"

"Oh, you know how it goes. Both of us were pretty busy. I'd say I'd maybe get over here two or three times a year, usually the holidays, and she'd come to Waseca about the same, but we talked on the phone just about every week. We'd check in. Since I've been living on my own, Anne's been real good to me."

"Just you two in the family?"

"Oh, no. We got two brothers in between us, but they moved away. One's out in California. The other's down in Florida. They don't stay in touch. You know how guys are."

Claire could see that Colette was calming down. She had eaten some of her pie and was sipping her coffee. So Claire decided to launch into the more tricky questions. "I'd like to ask you a few more questions about your sister's state of mind. What did Anne tell you was going on with her and Chet?"

"She wasn't specific, you know. Just kind of hinting around, like they were having some kind of sex problems."

Claire suddenly remembered a snippet of a conversation with Anne about a month ago. They had walked out to Anne's garden to look at her roses. Anne had said something about all things ending, even passion. She had said it in a funny way, looking at the full-blown rose in her hand. "Too much? Too little?"

"I got the feeling too little."

"According to whom?"

"Whom? What are you, some kind of professor? According to her, obviously. Otherwise, I probably wouldn't know about it. She didn't go into any gory details, but I could tell."

"Did she sound very upset about it? Did she think her husband was stepping out on her?"

Colette pursed her lips. "No, nothing like that. Just sounded like they were having problems."

"Did she seem depressed to you?" Claire asked.

"Hard to say. More like confused and a little angry. Like what about her, what was she supposed to do?" Colette pushed at her pie with her fork. "Our parents were totally stoics. Taught us not to complain when things were going wrong. Said nobody wants to hear your bad news. Hard to unlearn those sorts of lessons. So I was surprised when Anne even told me she was having a hard time. Especially about sex. To tell you the truth, I didn't want to know much more about it. Never asked her specifically what was wrong. Now I wish I did."

"You didn't get the feeling she was upset enough for her to kill herself?"

"No way." Colette slammed her fork down on her plate. "I'm sure she didn't. I already told you. I suppose it could have been Chet. Maybe she was too demanding. Maybe he was ashamed of not being able to take care of her. How do you expect me to know? Are you going to arrest him?"

"Well, he's in the hospital and a guard is there."

"Here? Why is he in the hospital?"

A twinge of guilt pricked Claire as she explained, "He tried to kill himself this morning." Claire thought of Chet sleeping in the hospital floors above them. The nurse had called earlier to say he had come around and was talking so Claire had sent over a deputy to sit watch. She wasn't going to make that mistake again.

Claire watched as Colette's face broke open, mouth hanging open, eyes pulling wide, nostrils flaring. Then she said, "I can't believe it. When did that happen? Was it one of those joint affairs where they tried to go together?"

"No, he did it a few hours…"

Before Claire could finish, Colette stood up as if she was going to leave, then turned back. "What's going on here? I know Anne and Chet were having some problems, but what happened to them that they would do this to each other?"

• • •

Definitely too hot to cook, Rich thought as he peered into the refrigerator. At ninety-three degrees, it was almost too hot to eat.

He decided to just make a salad. A big salad, full of tomatoes and peppers and cucumbers and throw in a can of tuna for protein. He could put in some of the green beans he had picked in Chet's garden. He figured as long as he was over there, he might as well harvest some of the veggies, otherwise they'd just go to waste.

Rich had gone back to feed Bentley for a second time. This time the dog hadn't raised a fuss at all. In fact, Bentley just slobbered over him. The horses had been let out to pasture and then back in. The chickens were back in their coop. A little early but he didn't want to have to go over there again today.

He put a small pan of water on to cook the beans and let them cool. He'd wait to see the whites of Claire's eyes before he'd throw the salad together.

While he was waiting, he grabbed a Leinenkugel's beer and sat on the deck where he could catch a breeze and watch for her car. The sun had dropped behind the trees that shaded the house to the west. Rich kicked his shoes off and stretched out full-length on a lawn chair.

The beer hit the spot. He liked to drink it ice cold and kept a couple mugs in the freezer just to keep it that way.

Rich remembered the first time he and Chet had gotten drunk. Chet stole a couple six-packs from his dad's fridge, the one he kept out in the garage that was just for beer. Figured his dad would never miss them.

All of fourteen years old, they had ridden their bikes down to the Rush River, brought their fishing rods, stuck the beers in the ice-cold spring water, which was always a cool forty-five degrees and started drinking. Two trout later, they had finished the first six-pack. Rich felt like his stomach was about to burst.

Then Chet fell into the river. It was too early in the season for the cold water to feel good. Rich started laughing and he tipped over the bucket and the two trout flapped their way back into the water.

When Chet managed to clamber back out of the river, they decided it was time to go home. The light was fading and the temperature was dropping. Neither one of them wanted to drink the last beers so they left them in the river. Too drunk to ride their bikes home, they had to walk, stopping for each other to throw up in the bushes. By the time they reached Chet's house, they were freezing and starving and hungover.

When they came walking up, Chet's dad had just stuck out his hand and asked for the money for the two six-packs, then he gave Rich a lift home. Rich's parents never said anything. Since he went right to bed, there was a chance they never knew, but he had a feeling his uneven walk and the smell probably gave him away.

The phone rang as he topped off his mug. He had to haul himself out of the lawn chair and walk into the kitchen to answer it.

"Yeah," he said.

"Rich, Jim Turner here."

"Hey, Jim, what can I do you for?"

"Just heard the news about Chet. Couldn't make heads or tails of it. Figured you'd have the inside scoop and all with Claire in the know. I heard he shot his wife, then tried to kill himself."

"What? Where'd you hear that?"

"Niece of mine works at the hospital. She said they brought him in early this morning. Guess he tried to hang himself in the jail of all places. Said his wife's laid out down in the morgue. What the hell's going on here, Rich? Can you give me the low-down?"

Rich took a moment to recover, then scrambled for something coherent to say. "First of all, Jim, no one knows what happened to Anne. I, for one, am sure that Chet didn't kill her. And I'm kind of in a spot here. Claire doesn't like me to talk about her work and all. Sounds like you know what there is to know."

"So it's true."

"You know as much as I do," Rich said, thinking, actually you know more than I do.

When he hung up, Rich stood at the railing and wondered if it was true. Could Chet really have tried to kill himself? He kept seeing his friend pitching horseshoes, hollering, "that's a ringer." Always ready to play a game, always wanting to win, always thinking things would turn out for the best. How could such a man try to kill himself?

Damn that woman, why hadn't Claire told him?

CHAPTER 10

Amy stood on the other side of Claire's desk, excited to tell her what they had found. She was sure the shirt would crack this John Doe case wide open. Claire was working on her computer. Amy waited until she looked up.

"Hey, Amy. What's up?"

"I had to tell you what we found down in a dumpster at the Maiden Rock park." Amy tried to slow herself down, but the words just came pouring out. "There's a chance it might not be anything. We don't know if this has anything to do with our John Doe, but it sure looks like it." Amy brought out the t-shirt that she had bagged.

"A t-shirt?" Claire looked at the large, dirty red t-shirt that Amy was holding out to her in a super-sized baggie.

"I think it might be from our guy. This tree symbol on the front matches the tattoo on his shoulder. Sven at the bar there remembers the guy wearing this t-shirt coming in for a drink and his description matches our guy too. Seems too close to be a coincidence."

Claire nodded. "Sounds good."

Amy went on. "So what I'm thinking is the guy was probably dumped there in Maiden Rock bay."

"Near where we found him?"

"Exactly." Amy pulled up a chair and started to explain, the words tumbling out of her in a torrent. "And in a way it makes a lot of sense. See, I checked the maps and the currents in Lake Pepin are slower than the rest of the river, and they're even slower in the bay areas, like near to where the body was found. There the current speed drops to about a half a foot a second. You can walk faster than that. Which isn't taking into account the eddies and all. What it was saying to me was that the body might not have been dumped very far from where it was found. Especially as the body might have been in the water as little as three to four days. Especially with this heat. You know decomposition happens fast when it's this hot."

Claire's face was blank, but Amy could tell she was listening carefully. Claire asked, "And be that bloated?"

"Well, the medical examiner explained to me how in this weather everything happens a lot faster. The water temperature in the lake is getting mighty close to eighty degrees and with the heat on the surface, the body would start to decompose very fast."

"Okay, then what did you figure?"

"Well, Bill and I…"

"Oh, Bill went with you?"

"Yes, and it was a good thing he did too, Claire. I couldn't have done it on my own."

Amy then proceeded to tell Claire in great detail about checking out the dock and then discovering the t-shirt and then going to the bar and finding out about the tree removal guy.

"So what do you think?" Amy asked when she could think of nothing else she needed to tell Claire.

"Amy, you're running with this case. I've got my hands full with the Baldwins. What do you think?"

Amy loved it when Claire asked her what she thought she should do. It showed her how much Claire thought of her ideas. She tried to be always ready for that question from Claire.

Amy had given it some thought and was glad to explain what she thought her next few steps should be. "First, I suppose we should send the t-shirt to the lab to see if they can find anything on it, like maybe some blood splatters. It's a little odd that there isn't a hole in it, but I thought about that and he was shot pretty low in the belly, right around the groin area, and maybe the shirt was pulled up or something.

"Then, I thought I'd check the computer for Minnesota tree service companies along the river, like in Red Wing and Hastings. There can't be too many. And then call them and see if they take jobs across the river and if any of their workers are missing."

Claire tapped her pencil on a pad of paper in a quick rhythm. "Have you checked missing persons for Minnesota?"

"Yes, but nothing's popped up. It can take a few days for the new cases to get entered. That's what I've been finding out."

"A tree removal guy. Seems kind of strange. What might he have done to get himself killed?"

"Maybe cut down the wrong tree?" Amy suggested.

Claire laughed. "Doesn't seem like it would be something to get killed over."

"Maybe when he was walking through the woods, marking trees to cut, he found something else, a secret. Or maybe he was in the wrong place at the wrong time and someone was hunting squirrel and shot him?"

"With a revolver? Not what guys usually hunt squirrels with."

"What do you think?" Amy asked.

"I think you've more than earned your pay today. I like where you're headed with this, Amy. Sounds like our John Doe is going to have a real name very soon. Please keep me posted."

Just what Amy was hoping she'd say.

• • •

Sheriff Talbert was leaning back in his chair, looking as tired and ornery at the end of the day as he ever did. Claire couldn't help noticing from time to time that his hair was getting sparser and his stomach was growing larger.

"Claire, I'm getting too old for this job," he said while rubbing his stomach. He had never been self-conscious about his weight—or anything else, for that matter.

"Don't you dare quit. You're only ten years older than me."

"But a lot goes downhill in those ten years, let me tell you."

"Is that why you called me in here, to complain about how old you're getting, Stewy?"

"I thought I'd start with the complaints. No really, I got some lab results I want to go over with you."

"Since when do you look at the lab results?"

He had the grace to look sheepish. "Oh, I can't help myself. I'm feeling pretty caught up in this investigation with Chet Baldwin. I mean he's been a friend for yea these many years. I didn't know him like Rich did. They're a little younger than me, went to school together, but since Chet's been on the county board I've worked with him closely on a couple projects. Nothing but admiration for that guy. When he says something, he does it."

"Can't argue with that."

"I'm just having a hard time believing he'd shoot anyone, let alone Anne. That's what I wanted to talk to you about."

Claire folded herself into a chair and waited. "You have my full and undivided attention."

"They've come up with a trace of someone else's blood from the living room rug. And it's not Chet's."

"Now you really do have my attention. How did the lab get the blood results so fast?"

"This is a simple blood test—just the blood type. Anne was O positive, Chet is B positive, and this other splotch of blood was B negative."

"What's going on here? Usually I'm giving you the information. Don't you think I'm handling this case correctly?"

Sheriff stretched his hands across the desk. "Don't go getting your panties in a twist, Claire. This isn't about you, it's about me. I know I'm meddling. I already said that. I just can't believe Chet would do such a thing."

Claire calmed herself down. She didn't need to get in a snit with the Sheriff. She sat down and he handed her the lab results. "O positive, very common, 37 percent of population has that. B positive, not so common at 10 percent. But this B negative is really rare, only one person in fifty has it. Might tell us something. But who else would have been in the house?"

The sheriff tapped the lab results with his forefinger. "It's worth checking out."

"So now you think we need to look for someone else?"

"What we need to do is get Chet here and hash it out with him. Find out what went on. Keep an open mind about what might have happened."

"Well, I certainly agree with that. I've made arrangements to pick him up tomorrow when he's released. In the meantime, one of the guys is parked outside his room."

"What does Rich have to say about this?" the sheriff asked. "He and Chet were best buds."

Claire said, "To tell you the truth, Stewy, we haven't talked about it much. I haven't been home. We talked on the phone, but I haven't even dared tell him about Chet's suicide attempt yet. He can't believe Chet would kill his wife. I don't really want to be the person to persuade him that it's a possibility. That's all there is to it."

•   •   •

When he came close to chopping a finger off as he cut up the carrots, Rich knew how upset he was. He tried to rein himself in, advising himself to give Claire a chance to explain when she got home, not to jump to any conclusions.

Resentment, he decided, was a good word to describe what he was feeling: resentment bordering on real anger. He was tired of how Claire was treating him, tired of how she just expected him to be there, supporting her, keeping the house running and her daughter attended to. Not that he didn't enjoy doing most of it, but he wouldn't mind a little acknowledgment once in a while.

And now she couldn't even call him and tell him when one of his best friends had tried to kill himself. How could she do that to him? How could she not take care of Chet and let him know what was going on?

She usually got home around six and here it was nearly seven o'clock. He was starving and decided to wait no longer. Rich poured the dressing over the salad and tossed it.

He was just getting ready to take his first bite when she walked in the door. He set down his fork.

"Hey, sorry, things piled up. Crazy day. That looks great." She sat down and started to dish up some salad. "Where's Meg?"

"She and Curt went to the county fair." Trying to contain his anger, he asked her, "Why didn't you tell me what happened to Chet? Jim Turner called and asked me what was going on with Chet. Hell if I know."

She looked at him, then tilted her head down. "Shit, Rich. I'm sorry. I just didn't want to go into it over the phone."

He hated that she said that to him. As if she could save him from something. In the past, she would have taken the time to tell him, even if it was over the phone. "So I have to hear about it from Jim? Do you know how that made me feel?"

"How did Jim know?"

"Claire, you're missing the point. News gets around here. You know that. You should have been the one to tell me." Rich pushed his plate away. He wasn't hungry anymore. "What happened?"

"You know, it's looking like he's going to be fine. Really." Claire rushed on, as if afraid that if she stopped she wouldn't be able to say it all. "I feel like it's my fault. I don't know what I was thinking last night. Maybe it's because he's a friend and that goofed me up too—but I just didn't think he'd try something like this. Chet always seems so capable."

"God, Claire, his wife is dead. What were you thinking?"

"I know, I know. I went and checked on him this morning at the hospital and the nurse called me later today. He's doing pretty good. Don't think there'll be any permanent damage. But he did try to hurt himself."

"Hurt himself? Is this the latest euphemism for trying to commit suicide?" Rich could feel himself getting mad. It didn't happen very often, but when it did he had a hard time controlling it. "How could that happen? Don't you watch for things like that? Wasn't that the whole point of you taking him in?"

"You think you're telling me something I don't know? I already said I made a mistake. I don't want to talk about it anymore. We've found out a few things, but I'd rather not talk about it."

"I think it's because you've already made your mind up about him. You are so sure that he killed Anne that you don't really care what happens to him."

"I am not sure. If there's one thing I know it's not to jump to conclusions, but I should remind you that even though he's your friend, he might have killed his wife. You don't know that side of people like I do."

"What about the forensic stuff? What's it showing?"

"Nothing that I can talk about."

Rich decided he needed to keep quiet. He shoved some food in his mouth, hoping it would keep him from saying anything more.

But after he had swallowed, the words just popped out. "Oh, so now you can't tell me about what you're working on. Usually I can't get you to quit. Whether I want to hear them or not. But when it's about someone who's my friend, who I care about, you decide it should be all hush-hush. So I have to hear about it from Jim and act like I already know. You should have called me the first thing."

"Rich, you need to calm down."

He pushed back his chair and stood up. "No, I don't think I do. I've been putting up with your rules for too long. Just because you're a deputy doesn't mean you make the laws in this house."

"I'm just trying to keep the peace."

"That's a good one." Rich felt like if he stayed in the house with Claire any longer he would say some things he would always regret. Better to get out. "I'm going to go and stay at Chet's tonight. The least I can do for the guy is take care of his animals and watch out for things until he gets back."

"Until he gets back? Rich, he tried to kill himself. That's a pretty good indication that he's guilty. So who knows when or if he will ever get out? Plus, you can't stay in the house. It's a crime scene."

"If you're trying to make me feel better, you're not succeeding. You seem to have made up your mind about Chet, but I haven't heard that you have any hard evidence or a confession. I'm sure you'd tell me if you did. I'll stay in the guest cabin that's behind his barn. Don't worry about your precious crime scene."

Rich went upstairs and gathered a few toiletries together in his Dopp kit, grabbed a clean t-shirt and some other clothes and shoved them in a bag.

Claire came and stood in the doorway and watched him. Then she said, "I have some good news. I'm not pregnant."

Rich turned, wondering what she was up to now, if she was serious. "Did you think you were?"

"Slight possibility."

"But you didn't think I needed to know that either? What's with you? Why didn't you tell me?"

"Wanted to be sure. No need for two of us to worry."

Sometimes she really didn't know him at all. "Claire, I wouldn't have been worried."

"Well, then I have bad news."

"What?"

"I think I'm starting into menopause."

He almost laughed, but turned the sound into a cough. Like this was news to him. "I figured."

"You did?"

"I read some article on the signs and you were showing a lot of them." He turned his back on her to finish packing.

Her voice cracked out. "Like what?"

"Like that. Snapping at me. Not sleeping very well. Hotter than a furnace. You never used to sweat. Now sometimes the sweat rolls off you like a farm worker. I vaguely remember my mother having similar problems."

"That's real nice. First you say I sweat and then you compare me to your mother. What other complaints do you have?"

"I wasn't complaining. Just some things I've noticed."

"Do you think you can handle it?"

"Do I have a choice?"

"Yeah, you could walk out on me and find a younger woman."

"I'll think about it." Rich walked down the stairs with his bag and she followed him.

"Rich, you don't have to go," Claire said.

"We need a break. This way I can keep an eye on his place. Who knows what someone might try to do if they know no one's there. Tell Meg she should do the morning feed for the pheasants."

"Rich," Claire said again.

He was glad to hear a slight pleading in her voice, but he was sure of what he needed to do.

When he got to the door, he turned and said to her, "Claire, if I were going to hook up with someone else, I wouldn't go younger. I think I'd try an older woman. One who's already done with this shit."

He let the door slam behind him. He knew she hated that sound.

CHAPTER 11

Where's Rich?" Meg asked, standing in the kitchen doorway in cut off shorts and an undershirt. She wiped her eyes and looked around the kitchen. "He usually makes the coffee, not you. Is he sick?"

"No. You're up early," Claire said after checking the kitchen clock, which read 7:05. Her daughter had caught her anxiously watching the coffee drip through the filter into the waiting pot. This morning she desperately needed a hit of coffee. She hadn't been able to sleep but a few hours last night. She had to think over all Rich said to her about a million times, wondering and hoping that he might be right about Chet, worrying that her negligence had caused Chet's suicide attempt.

"You want a cup of coffee?" she asked her daughter.

"Where'd he go? He knows how to make my coffee just the way I like it—better than Starbucks."

"He's very temporarily staying up at Chet's."

Meg plopped down in a chair at the kitchen counter. "What? Do you mean he moved out? Why?"

"Because I'm a self-centered bitch who always thinks she's right."

"He just noticed?" Meg chuckled. "Seriously, where is he?"

"Seriously, he's at Chet's. He needed a break from me. I don't blame him. I can hardly stand me." Claire was embarrassed to feel tears threatening.

"Oh, Mom, don't be so hard on yourself." Meg walked over and, standing shoulder to shoulder with her mother, wrapped an arm around her. "But you have been a little crabby lately. Even Curt noticed."

"Don't tell me that. I can't help it. It's not my fault." Claire snuffled back the tears. The last thing she needed to do was break down in front of her daughter. She couldn't believe how emotional she felt all the time.

"Whose fault is it?" Meg backed off and returned to her chair. "Don't say it's mine, because, one, I've been in a cheerful mood, and, two, I even cleaned my room. I don't know if you've noticed."

"It's certainly not your fault. No, it's just one of those things."

"What things?"

"You probably don't want to hear about this, but I think I'm going into menopause. Your mom's turning into an old lady." The coffee was finally ready so Claire poured herself a cup of coffee and offered the pot to Meg.

"We studied that in health at the end of last year. I don't know how they expect us to remember all this stuff since it's like a million years away. But menopause doesn't sound good. It's like your bones start to crumble and your mind disintegrates." After pouring herself a slug of coffee, Meg started to add other ingredients to the cup: sugar, milk, then some cocoa.

"Yeah, that's it. That's what's happening to me." Claire popped some bread into the toaster. "Rich just needed a breather. Anne's death has been very hard on both of us."

"You guys were pretty good friends, weren't you?"

Claire thought about Meg's question. "I guess. We really liked each other. I wouldn't say I felt like I knew her really well. She was younger and more of a housewife than I am. They had that big farm to run: her horses, the dog. But when we got together it was always fun. Chet and Rich were the true friends."

"Maybe you should marry Rich so he can't leave you. Just a suggestion in case you never thought about it."

"I don't think that makes any difference." Claire wanted to change the subject. "How's your darling Curt?"

"He's scrumptious. Isn't he the nicest guy, Mom?" Meg smiled up at her with a dark moustache of cocoa powder.

"Lick your lip, honey. Yes, he's pretty darn nice."

"Weird to meet someone that nice when I'm this young. I mean, what am I supposed to do if he's the love of my life? I mean, it's years before I'd even want to think of marrying someone. A girl's gotta see a little action."

"What does that mean?" Claire gave her a sharp look.

"Don't worry, we haven't done anything serious yet. We're still in the talking about it phase."

"Good. Stay in that phase for about the next four years."

"Seriously, Mom, when did you have sex for the first time?"

The toast popped up and Claire grabbed for it. "I don't think I have time for this conversation this morning, darling daughter. And I'm not sure you need to have that information, but I will tell you this—I wasn't barely sixteen years old."

. . .

Unable to sleep in the heat, Amy woke up early and decided to go into the department where there was air-conditioning. As she threw off the sheet, she thought of Bill's place. It had air-conditioning, but they weren't quite at the point of spending every night together.

There was no food in her apartment so she stopped and picked up a cup of bad coffee at the gas station and a soggy donut. This dismal breakfast would keep her going for a while.

Amy was glad to get in early, because she was determined to find the tree guy and she felt like she could only devote a day to it. The sheriff's department was quiet, a few guys around.

She got on the computer and typed in: Minnesota + "tree services." Fifty thousand hits came up on Google. Trying to narrow it down, she typed in: Minnesota + "tree removal services." Not much better. Thirty thousand hits. So she decided she better start close to home. If the tree guy was from Minnesota he was probably from either Wabasha or Red Wing; maybe Lake City, possibly Hastings. She also figured that there was a good chance he owned the company—few employees showed such dedication to their place of employment as to have it tattooed on their arm.

Amy started with Red Wing, which was at the north end of the lake, and only about fifteen miles away from the top of Pepin County. Rather than using Google she'd try the phone book. After scouting around the office, she found a year-old Red Wing phone book.

There were six tree service companies. She decided to start with Red Wing Tree Removal Services. Pretty straight forward. Even though it was seven in the morning, she figured it wasn't too early to call. Tree guys would be on farm time.

An answering service picked up. She left a message.

The second company she tried—Halsten Bros. Tree Trimmers—she got a person on the other end of the line. "Yes, I'm wondering if you do work in Wisconsin?"

"Depends," the gruff man's voice answered. "Where you at?"

"Pepin."

"Sure, we go over that a way. What's your problem?"

"Well, actually I'm calling from the sheriff's department of Pepin County. I'm Deputy Amy Schroeder. I'm trying to track down a missing person and I'm wondering if any of your workers have gone missing."

"Are you serious? Is this for real?"

"Yes, sir. We have found a body of a man in Lake Pepin and have reason to believe that he might have been working for a tree removal company."

"Geez, I read about that yesterday in the paper. It's just me and my brother working together. I saw my brother yesterday so I know he hasn't gone missing. Once in awhile, if we get real busy we hire some extra hands, but we don't have anyone else right now. Don't think I can be much help."

"Before I let you go, can I ask you one more question?"

"Shoot."

"Do you know a tree guy who wears a red t-shirt with the logo of a tree on it?"

Silence for a moment, then, "Doesn't ring a bell."

"Well, thank you anyway."

Amy wrote the name of the company down and put a check next to it. She had a feeling it was going to be a long day.

•   •   •

Claire ended up spending most of the morning at her desk, filling out paperwork from the latest break-in in town, which had happened a few days before the floater was found. Since meth had hit their small county, break-ins had become much more frequent.

When she called the hospital, they said Chet Baldwin would be ready to leave later in the day. Claire asked to speak to his nurse.

When the woman came on, Claire asked, "How's he doing?"

"Still rather out of it. We've tapered off the sedative. He seems to be coming around. The psychiatrist was in this morning and he felt that Mr. Baldwin could leave the hospital as long as he was being watched. The endoscopy came back showing minimal damage to his throat and larynx. So he should be good to go." There was a pause on the other end of the line. "He seems like such a nice guy. Did he really kill his wife and then try to kill himself?"

"He hasn't been charged with a crime—we're still looking into it." Claire caught herself wanting to spout some babble like even good people can do bad things, but she simply thanked the nurse and said she'd be there to pick him up at three.

After going out on a call—an older woman in Durand had

had her garden tore up by some kids—Claire came back to the department and checked in with the hospital again. This time the nurse on duty said Mr. Baldwin was ready to be released.

Claire asked to talk to the deputy on duty there, who turned out to be Pete. When he came to the phone, she asked him how Chet seemed.

"He's moving kinda slow, but he's moving."

Kinda slow actually described Pete. He was a hulk of a man who didn't do anything fast. "You're just about to go off duty, aren't you, Pete?"

"Yeah."

"Why don't you bring him down to the lobby and wait for me. I'll pick him up and you can go on home."

When she walked into the hospital, Claire saw Chet sitting in a wheelchair by the front desk and Pete, all two hundred and fifty pounds of him, standing right next to him, one hand on the grip of the chair.

Chet looked up as Claire walked over, his head rising slowly on the stalk of his thin neck. She was surprised by how pasty his face was. Bruising still circled his neck and he sat hunched over in the wheelchair, looking like he belonged in it.

Chet was a tall, lanky man. Claire had always thought of him as strong and agile, outdoor work and hunting kept him in good shape. But today he looked old and decrepit.

"How're you feeling?" she asked him.

He reached out his hand toward her in an informal shake.

She took his hand and he gave it a tentative squeeze, again not the usual Chet handshake.

"Not great. Claire, I'm sorry to be putting you in this position. I feel awful. The doctors tell me I did quite a number on myself. What was I thinking?"

"Well, let's go back to the government center and we can talk about what has happened. We've got a therapist coming in to see you."

"Oh, now, I don't need anyone like that. I just want to go home. Can you take me home?"

"Chet, you're in no shape to go home. We need to talk to you about what happened to Anne." Claire dropped his hand. She was paying attention to the way he had phrased that last sentence he said to her before he had tried to hang himself: *all my doing,* but not *I did it.* Big difference there. "Wait until we're back at the sheriff's department."

Chet's head came up and he said with some feeling, "Claire, for god's sake, don't act like you don't know me. You've had dinner at my house. I'm not going anyplace. You'll hear the whole story. But right now I really need to go home. Could you just take me back?"

Claire didn't want to get into it with him in the hospital. She nodded at the deputy, who now had both hands on the wheelchair grips and was ready to push the wheelchair. "Let's go. I'm parked right out front."

When they got to the squad car, Chet stood and made a move to sit in the front seat, but Claire ushered him into the back. She didn't want to take any chances with Chet this time. She would bring him in right and by the book.

As she drove him the few blocks to the government center, he asked if Rich had been feeding the animals.

"Oh, yeah. In fact, he's staying in your cabin to keep an eye on things." Claire hoped he wouldn't ask any questions about that.

"Oh, geez, he didn't have to do that."

"Well, it just worked out for him."

"If you'd just take me home, I could take care of everything. Rich doesn't need to be there."

Claire parked right in front of the door to the sheriff's department and, as the back doors were locked, walked around the car to open the door.

When she pulled the car door open, Chet erupted from the seat and shoved into her as hard as he could.

Totally taken by surprise, Claire went flying and landed on her butt while Chet took off running across the parking lot. As she scrambled to her feet, he disappeared into the woods.

CHAPTER 12

By the time Claire got back to her feet, Chet had disappeared into the woods on the far side of the parking lot.

Claire stopped for a moment to think about where he was headed. The woods were just tucked into the side of the hill. At most they covered an area of about an acre, an overgrown couple of lots on a hill that backed down into town, with Highway 25 at the bottom.

She knew she should call for backup, but there was no time. Claire had to catch Chet before he got too far away. Even though he had a head start, she figured he had to be somewhat slowed down by his hospital stay. She took off across the parking lot after him.

Claire swore under her breath as she plunged into the thicket of locust and oak with a dense understory of gooseberries and raspberries, all of them tearing at her pants. She couldn't see him, but could hear wood snapping and crashing ahead of her as he forced his way through the tangle.

"Chet, stop," she hollered as she ran, surprised by how winded she already was. Then, louder, "Chet, this isn't the way."

She stopped yelling. He wasn't listening to her. It was clear he had been planning this escape all along. She was wasting her breath. Trying to avoid low branches, she stooped as she ran.

As she neared the far side of the woods, she caught a glimpse of the white of his shirt as he broke out of the woods. Once he hit the highway, it would be clear sailing for him, easy to run along the sidewalk or disappear into the town. She wanted to catch him before he got across the traffic.

Claire put on a burst of speed and came out of the woods right behind him.

Chet was stalled out on the side of the road, waiting for traffic to clear. At least that's what Claire thought he was doing at first. He glanced back at her and jumped forward just as a large delivery truck came speeding down the highway in the outside lane. It looked like Chet stepped out into the highway, purposefully putting himself right in its path.

Claire came up behind him. She lunged at him and grabbed the back of his shirt, pulling him backward, barely out of the way. Chet fell toward her and hit Claire hard, right in the chest, causing her to lose her balance.

Her left arm shot out to break her fall and hit the edge of the curb, taking her full weight as she crashed down with Chet on top of her.

A bolt of pain shot up her arm and then burst in her head. It was unlike anything she had felt before. She rolled over onto her back, looking up at the blue sky with a burning, tearing sensation radiating out from her arm. She sucked in air. Scared to look at her hurt limb, she lay still for a moment. When she tried to push herself up with her other arm, it hurt too much to move.

Chet stood over her, looking down with concern. "Sorry," he said, then reached down as if to help her up.

She didn't want him to touch her. He might hurt her even more. She couldn't stand that thought. "Don't," she said.

He shook his head and took off running across the highway.

Claire stayed sitting on the sidewalk, surprised that no one was stopping to check on her. At least she was out of the way of traffic. She felt her arm and didn't like how sore it was. She was afraid she had done some serious damage to it. Sweat poured off her body and she felt sick to her stomach, but held it in.

Breathe from your belly, she told herself. You need to take care of yourself. Panic will not help the situation. You're going to need to get on your feet somehow. Stay calm. Breathe.

Chet was long gone. Forget about him. She needed to get her arm checked out by a doctor.

No one was stopping. She couldn't just sit there, waiting for someone to help her. She had to get herself back to the government center. She thought of trying to flag a car down, but the center was only a block away, up a hill. This time she wouldn't cut through the woods. She could make it.

She needed to stabilize her arm and the only way to do that was to wrap her other arm around it. She reached over with her good right arm and gently moved her broken arm in closer to her body. Any jolt to it sent pain washing through her.

Claire undid the two buttons of her shirt above her pants. As carefully as she could she slid her broken arm into the opening of her shirt. Then she rolled to her side and up onto her haunches.

She rocked in a squat position, waiting for the nausea to subside. She pushed herself up and stood, hanging her head, breathing deeply. She never knew pain came in so many colors. They rolled through her head as she tried to ride out this latest surge.

Cupping her left elbow in her right hand, she cradled the injured arm. For a moment, she felt okay. She felt hope. It might be possible to walk up the hill if she took it very slowly.

Claire knew that in the first few minutes after an accident, the victim usually didn't realize how badly they were hurt. She hated to think that her arm was worse than she thought. Or maybe her body had skipped that step. Not fair.

She held her injured arm right against her body and took a step. It was tolerable. Slow and steady. Never jerking. Pushing up the hill, step by step, slowly but steadily. No movement that would jar her arm.

Claire was sure it would take forever to walk up the hill. Here she had a man on the lam and she couldn't even manage the few steps back to the department to call out the forces.

When she saw the government center and knew she would make it, she almost sat down with relief. But instead she leaned against a tree and kept her sight on the parking lot, the building.

As Claire stepped onto the tarmac, someone came out of the building. She stopped and waited for them to see her. The person waved. She could tell it was a man, a deputy in uniform, not sure who it was, couldn't tell. She stayed holding her arm in place.

He looked over at her and she tried to motion with her good arm but it hurt to much to move anything.

"Hey," she yelled. "Help."

As the man got closer, she could see that it was Jeremy. He started to run toward her and she got scared of what he might do.

"Jeremy," she yelled again.

"What's the matter?"

"He got away. Chet ran away."

"But what happened to you?"

As he got closer, she stuck out her good arm to stop him. "Don't touch me. I'm afraid it's broken."

Jeremy stopped and stared at her, his mouth slightly hanging open. "How'd you do that?"

"Jeremy, now's not the time. I need to get to the hospital. And you need to let the sheriff know about Chet."

"Can you walk?" he asked.

She could see his face, his mouth moving, but she didn't really know what he was saying. "Oh, yeah. I'm fine."

Claire took a step toward him. He shut his mouth and reached for her. That was the last thing she remembered.

•   •   •

Bentley raced ahead as Rich walked down the field road that cut through Chet's property. Rich had opened the pasture gate and the two horses, all on their own, galloped back to the barn. They'd be waiting for him when he got there. He skirted the perimeter of the property, just to get a little walk in. Bentley seemed enthusiastic about the idea, tearing ahead of him, then trotting back to see what was keeping him.

Rich walked toward the woods, hoping to find some shade. The record-breaking heat wave was showing no signs of abating. Mid-nineties again today. The fields were turning brown a little earlier than usual because of the dryness and heat.

Grasshoppers whirred up around him as he walked through

the tall grasses. Clicking sounds filled the air. Bentley snapped at the grasshoppers, then he'd shake his head if he caught one. Must not taste too good.

Rich was torn about going back to his house for the night. He had stopped by around mid-day and checked on the pheasants, had a peanut butter and jelly sandwich with Meg, and picked up another clean t-shirt and boxer shorts just in case he decided to stay on at Chet's.

Meg had asked him when he was coming back. He told her in the next few days. As soon as Chet was home again. When she asked him what was going on between him and her mother, he tried to sidestep the question, but she stopped him.

"I know you guys are fighting. Mom told me she's turned into a bitch, plus I have eyes and ears you know."

"We just needed a little break, that's all. I love your mother, but she can get on my nerves."

"I know she's kinda bossy, but I think most of the time you like that about her. She knows what she wants and, for better or worse, I think she wants you."

He smiled at how blunt Meg could be. Just like her mom. Funny how much more tolerable it was in Meg, even admirable. A young girl needs all the attitude she can muster. "I do like how clear and straightforward Claire is but in this instance, I wish she'd try to see things in a different light."

"I told her that too. I think it's hard on her. In her job she has to be so decisive, everyone's counting on her."

"You're right, Miss Meg. But a few days apart won't hurt us."

"I hope not."

Rich stood staring over the fields and thinking of his life with Claire. It had been so full of promise when they met. Somehow he thought she would fit into his life more than she ever had—bake him a pie, go fishing with him, morel hunting, help him with the pheasants—be more of a partner to him. He had never wanted to turn her into a housewife, but he had thought she might integrate more into his concerns. It had taken him a long time to accept how all consuming her job was; how, even when she was home, it filled her thoughts.

He was never bored with Claire, but he wasn't often as content as he'd like to be sometimes. As he grew older, that quality seemed to grow in importance.

Bentley growled at something off in the weeds. Rich hoped he had been right in what he had said to Meg. He hoped that nothing basic in his relationship with Claire was being destroyed.

He followed Bentley and saw a path through the grasses as if a large vehicle had driven through recently. The grass was bent over and broken. The field sloped down into the woods and as they came over a rise, he saw what looked like a truck parked at the edge of the forest, hidden in sumac bushes.

Typical old farmer behavior. Truck doesn't work anymore, just drive it into the weeds and let it rust its little heart out. He hated that everyone still did that. Calling Bentley to him, he walked up closer to get a better look.

Rich pushed aside the hairy sumac branches and saw that the vehicle was a relatively new Chevy pickup, probably still worth some money. It wasn't Chet's truck, that he knew for sure—Chet was a Ford man. What would it be doing in his woods?

The grass had grown up around the tires and he could barely make out a path where the truck had driven into the woods. Didn't happen yesterday.

Maybe, during his walk, he had crossed over the property line. He wasn't sure exactly where Chet's property ended. But still, why would anyone dump a decent truck like that in the weeds? You'd think even if it didn't run anymore, a salvage company would come and pick it up just for parts.

One more thing he'd have to ask Chet about when he saw him next.

•   •   •

As the end of the day approached, Amy wasn't looking forward to going back to her hot apartment. Bill had already left, but she might have to call him up and bribe him with some ice cream to let her stay over. She had had no luck with the tree guy and was quite disappointed that her find hadn't panned out. Maybe a discarded red t-shirt is simply a discarded red t-shirt, not some clue to solve the crime of the year.

She had called all the tree services in Red Wing and the surrounding area. She had even gotten a call back from the two services she had left messages with. Everyone she talked to sounded disappointed when they found out she wasn't calling about needing any work done.

One of the owners had explained to her it had been a relatively quiet summer, not many storms, no tornadoes or straight-line winds, so there hadn't been as many felled trees as usual. As a result they weren't using many extra workers and none of them had any workers who were missing.

None of them knew anything about a red shirt with a tree on it. Maybe the tree guy was from Wisconsin after all. She thought to herself, *Maybe I'm barking up the wrong tree*, and had a short fit of hysterical laughter.

She was just about ready to give up when she picked up the Shopper and read an ad for a tree service located between Red Wing and Hastings. It was just a small note in the classifieds. Seemed odd for them to be advertising in a Wisconsin paper, but it answered her first question, which was "do you do work in Wisconsin?"

She called the listed number and a woman answered the phone, not with the name of the company, which was Timber Tree Services, but just a simple, "hello."

"Hi, is this Timber Tree Services?"

There was a pause and then the woman said, "My husband isn't available just right now."

"Oh, but he runs Timber Tree Services?"

"Yes, when he's around."

"May I ask where he is?"

"Who is this?" the woman's voice rose.

"Oh, sorry. I'm calling from the Pepin County Sheriff's Department. My name is Amy Schroeder."

"What do you want? Is there some problem?"

"I know this is an odd question, but does he have a red t-shirt with a tree on it?"

"He had a bunch of those shirts made up for him and the guys. Why?"

Amy sucked in her breath. "I need to talk to your husband. Do you know how I can get hold of him?"

"My husband's not here. He's been gone for nearly a week this time and I haven't heard a peep."

"Have you reported him missing?"

"Not worth the trouble. He'll show up in the next day or two with some lame excuse about where he's been. I don't get too worried about it. Is he in trouble or something?"

"What's your husband's name?"

"Dean Swaggum."

"Is he a big guy?"

"Yeah, weighs about two twenty, over six feet tall. Why?"

Amy was afraid to ask the next question, the make-it or break-it question. "Does he have a tattoo?"

The woman's voice quavered as she answered, "Yes. He got it when he started the business."

"May I ask what it is?"

"Why? What's happened to him?"

"Maybe nothing. Can you describe the tattoo?"

"A whole tree, not just the branches, but the roots too."

Amy sat stunned in her chair. Now what did she say? She had never broken the news of a death to someone before. She wished Claire were here. "Mrs. Swaggum, I'm afraid I'm going to have to ask you to come to Durand."

CHAPTER 13

Amy was sitting in front of the computer when she heard someone running in the main room. Bernice, the secretary, called out Claire's name. She heard someone say that Claire had been hurt, was in the parking lot passed out on the ground. Amy pushed her chair back so hard it tipped over and she ran out the door.

By the time she got there, Jeremy and three other deputies surrounded Claire. Amy pushed Jeremy away and squatted down to check on Claire. Her face was blotchy red and covered with sweat. She was unconscious, but breathing.

Then Amy saw what the problem was. Claire had tucked her arm in her shirt, but the break was so exaggerated that the arm bent where it shouldn't. At least it hadn't broken through the skin yet, but she could see the bone pushing against the forearm from the inside.

Frank pulled a squad car up as close as he could get to Claire and opened the back door. "Let's get her in here. No sense waiting for an ambulance. We can take her just as fast."

The four of them lifted Claire up and laid her in the back seat of the car. Amy got in from the other side and put Claire's head on her lap, trying to stabilize her body. "Let's go," she said.

"Just take it nice and easy."

Claire moaned and opened her eyes. "What?" she asked.

"You're going to be fine. We're taking you to emergency. Hang in there."

"Chet?" Claire said the word as if there was more.

"What about him?" Amy asked.

"Chet got away."

"He was with you?"

"He ran through the woods, then across the highway."

"Shit." Amy turned and said to Frank. "I think Chet Baldwin's loose. Maybe give a holler back to the department and let them know."

"He got away," Claire mumbled again.

"Don't worry. The guys will find him."

Reaching down with her good hand, Claire felt along her other arm. "I think it's broken."

"Looks like it."

Claire gave a wan smile. "At least it's my left. I can still write and drive."

"You might have to take some time off."

Claire shook her head. Then she touched her broken arm again. "I suppose they're going to have to straighten this out. Not looking forward to that."

•   •   •

"Claire was right here. Looks like he ran into the woods down there a ways." Bill pointed out a path in the underbrush.

Sheriff Talbert glanced up at the sky, then shook his head. "What the hell do we do now? We haven't arrested him, at least not formally. We need to talk to him, but I'm just not sure we should do a large-scale manhunt for Chet. Technically, no reason he couldn't walk off if he wanted to."

"But what about assaulting a deputy sheriff?" Bill asked, disappointed that he wasn't going to be allowed to organize a major search and concerned about the treatment of a fellow officer. "After all, Claire's got a broken arm."

"Did he do that?"

Bill had to admit he wasn't sure. "Where do you think he'd go?"

"Well, I'm sure he's headed home. But who knows, he might have gone downtown for a cup of coffee."

"Can't a few of us guys go looking for him?"

The sheriff motioned to him to head back to the government center. "I think that's a good idea. If nothing more than just to check on him and make sure he's all right. After all, he's tried to kill himself once. I'd suspect he might try again. In fact, you might want to go see if he's on the bridge over the Chippewa." Then the sheriff shook his head. "Although I don't think it's high enough to kill anybody if they went off of it. Who knows what he might try to do? I'd sure feel better if he was back here in our custody."

"Where would you suggest we start?" Bill held the door open for the sheriff who thanked him and walked through it.

"Geez, Chet could be anywhere." The sheriff thought about it for a moment, then continued, "If he makes his way over to the Tiffany Bottoms along the river, we'd never find him if he didn't want us to. In this warm weather he could stay out for weeks. Chet knows all this land around here like the back of his hand. He's hunted just about every square inch of it. And hunter that he is, he can live off the land for as long as he needs to."

"He's been gone about a half an hour." Bill looked at his watch. "Might not be in the best shape of his life after what he did to himself. I'm thinking we form a circle about four miles out from Durand and try to catch him that way."

"Wait a second here. First of all, I'd check a few places in town. Just to see if anyone has seen him. Don't go skipping over the easy stuff. Let's talk to Claire before we go off half-cocked."

"Gotcha."

"Now if he's serious about this—if he really wants to go disappear—it's not going to be easy to find him. He won't be on the roads or anything. He'll cut right through the woods. He can swim the Chippewa for that matter."

"How many deputies can I have to do this?"

"Why don't you take Frank, Red and Amy?"

"Frank and Amy took Claire to emergency."

"Well, they'll be back soon enough. Oh, in the meantime, why don't you take Jeremy?"

"Jeremy? He doesn't know his ass from a hole in the ground."

The sheriff shot him a look. "That's why this would be good for him, Bill. In fact, I'd like to see you take him under your wing. Teach him some of your good-old expertise."

Bill knew he should have kept his mouth shut.

"We don't need to go crazy, but try to find Chet." The sheriff leaned against the wall right outside his office and shook his head. "This isn't looking good for him, this running away."

• • •

Rich stretched out on the twin bed in the cabin and stared at the beadboard ceiling. How had he gotten here? Hard to backtrack and go home again after all he had said to Claire. Not that she made any big plea for him not to leave her, but she had tried to explain why she had waited to tell him about Chet.

His thoughts kept returning to Chet and Anne. Anne dead and Chet trying to kill himself. What had gone so very wrong? Rich hadn't seen Chet much lately, just the time of year, so much to do at the end of summer. Haying, getting the pheasants ready for market, harvesting the gardens.

The last time they had been together was down at the Fort. About a month or so ago, Chet had called him up and asked if he wanted to go have a beer or two and shoot some pool. They had played a few games, drank a couple brews, then sat and talked for a bit afterwards.

He didn't remember much of what they talked about, the usual—weather, crops, animals—but just as they were leaving, Chet had turned to him and said, "So how are things with you and Claire?"

The question had surprised him. They didn't tend to talk about their relationships. Rich had said fine.

Chet had taken a swig off his beer bottle, then asked, "You guys still getting some exercise in the sack?"

What a weird way to ask if they were having regular sex, Rich had thought at the time, plus, none of your business. He had nodded noncommittally.

"We've slacked off," Chet said.

Rich had mumbled something about getting older, these

things happen. Then he had asked Chet if he'd been doing any fishing.

Now he wished he had not changed the subject, but had asked Chet what was going on with them. The one thing he did know about his friend was how important the physical side of love was to him. Before Chet married Anne, he had had a number of woman friends, even some coming down from the Cities. He would mention from time to time how good they were in bed, not going into any gory detail, but letting Rich know that he was a satisfied man.

Rich wondered, as he had constantly for the last two days, what had happened the night Anne died, if it had had anything to do with the slacking off of sex between them. He just couldn't imagine Chet going to that length to get rid of her.

If she hadn't killed herself then it had to have been Chet who shot her. Rich supposed there was a possibility that someone had come over to the farm while Chet went for his walk and shot Anne and then Chet returned and thought she had killed herself. But not likely.

Trying to understand what happened to Chet and Anne—if their relationship could have gone so very wrong—Rich couldn't help but think about Claire. He knew it was to be expected that the sex thing died down a little, and actually that wasn't a big problem for him. They connected often enough for him to remember how intense it had once been. A mellower, gentler love-making suited him just fine.

What rubbed him the wrong way with Claire was that he felt taken for granted. Much of what he had admired about Claire when they first met had started to wear thin: how focused she was on her work, her need to always be right, the way she had to be in charge. Claire wasn't like that in bed—not that she was submissive, but she let him call the shots whenever he wanted to. Maybe that was what was important.

Just thinking about her in bed made him think it was time to head back home, at least for a night or two.

From his vantage point on the bed, Rich could see under the footstool on the opposite side of the small room. There was what looked like a crumpled Kleenex in the shadows.

Rich got off the bed and reached down to see what it was.

He was so shocked by what he found in his hand that he threw it back on the floor and said, "Goddamn, Chet! What were you thinking?"

Inside the Kleenex was a condom that had obviously been used.

CHAPTER 14

Durand was located about sixteen miles upriver from the mouth of the Chippewa River, at the point where it turned and headed south toward the Mississippi River. Chet stood in the shadow of a brick building just south of the Highway 10 bridge, facing the river. He needed to take a breather before his next move, which would be to cross the river.

A few cars were parked along the back street. Chet sank down in the shade of a big oak tree close to the river. He knew they would be looking for him. Claire hadn't followed him across the highway, he figured she had gone back for reinforcements. He hoped she hadn't been too hurt when she fell. What had he started? But he needed to get away from everyone and figure out what he was going to do.

The horrible thing was Claire thought he killed Anne. He wasn't sure he could dissuade her of that. He wasn't even sure he wanted to.

All Chet knew was he needed time to think. And he always thought well while walking in the woods. He could follow the Chippewa river down to the Tiffany Bottoms and disappear for a day or two. Just enough time to sort things out in his mind.

Figure out if it was even worth continuing to live in a world without Anne.

A fifteen minute rest was all he could afford to take. Chet checked the street behind him before he let himself stand up and walk down to the river. He followed the river out of town, heading southwest toward Lake Pepin, past the Bauer Built offices, then past the small subdivision of Pleasant Ridge to where the river curved away from the town and he would be out of sight of any houses.

When he was safely past the last house, he looked at what he was wearing, the clothes he had worn when Anne died: his wrinkled khaki pants, a light shirt and running shoes. He knew if he looked closely he'd find some spatters of blood, but he didn't want to see them.

He took his shoes off and tied the laces together, then hung them around his neck. They would get wet, but at least they wouldn't weigh his feet down. Chet strolled along the river bank. The silty sand was the color of the limestone bluffs that surrounded this area, golden creamy as butter.

The wet sand felt good on his feet. He used to go barefoot all summer long when he was a kid. What had happened to those carefree days? When had he stopped taking his shoes off?

The water was rushing past him like quicksilver. He rolled up his pants and walked in up to his knees. Cool but not cold. Even the fast, cold waters of the Chippewa had warmed up during this hot spell. He walked in further until the water was up to his waist, and then he dove in. He didn't make a great effort to get to the other side—he let the water sweep him along and carry him downstream. He turned over on his back and floated.

It was a nice way to travel. As he watched Durand disappear around a bend in the river, he was surprised at how quickly he was moving away.

Chet floated low in the water, which he had done since he was a skinny kid. Nose, mouth and chin stayed above water, eyes and chest if he lightly paddled. If anyone happened to see him, they might think he was a muskrat or a beaver, making a watery trail.

After about fifteen minutes in the river, he came to an island he recognized, close to Silver Birch Lake. He wanted to make it down to past Ella, where he could walk out and follow county road N past Little Plum Creek and down to Back Valley Road. He figured the river was flowing at about three miles an hour and if he gently swam along with it, he could travel about four to five miles an hour, which would put him at Ella in another hour or so.

He knew of an old shack just off of Swede Rambler Lane where he could camp out for a day or two. A friend of his used it for a hunting cabin, but Chet was sure no one was there now. It was only about a mile or so from the river. It wouldn't take him long to walk there and then he could rest. If he guessed right, there was probably a decent supply of canned goods to make something to eat.

As he did a lazy crawl down the river he thought of Anne.

If Anne were still alive they would be dancing right now. This was the afternoon that they went to the Moose Lodge to polka and waltz and fox trot. They had met dancing in Red Wing and it had continued to be a part of their lives together.

He swam close to the shore and watched the river birch glide by. No more dancing for him ever again.

• • •

Bill stood on the bridge and watched the water flow beneath him. This was the only bridge across the Chippewa for miles: about twelve miles downstream Highway 35 crossed it and then eight miles upstream there was another bridge. He was betting on Chet trying to come across the bridge.

Staring down into the water, Bill couldn't imagine anyone trying to cross the river by swimming. The current wasn't too strong, but the river was filled with debris and looked the color of weak coffee. Who knew what was in that dark brew: sewage, silt, and slimy carp.

Only problem was there was a small chance that Chet might have already crossed the bridge before Bill got to his post. It had taken him some time to gather the troops. He sent Jeremy south on Highway 25 in a squad car to watch the road. He asked Red to stay in town and ask people if they had seen Chet.

He had called Amy at the hospital and told her to join him on the bridge when she could get away. She said that Claire was doing fine. They had set her arm and given her one of those new-fangled plastic casts. The doctor had also given her a Vicodin. Amy laughed at that point and said Claire was feeling no pain. In fact, she said, Claire was talking on and on about all sorts of stuff, not all of which made any sense, but she seemed happy. Someone in her family was going to come and get her, Amy thought, but she'd stay until they showed up.

Sounded as if Claire might be out of commission for a while. He wasn't quite the next in command but he was getting up there. He was happy that the sheriff had put him in charge of this search party and the way he looked at it, if he caught Chet, then he might get to do more of this type of work. Maybe Claire would be so bad off that they'd make him temporary chief investigator. He hated to think that way, but he didn't see how else he'd advance as the department was so small. He'd thought of moving and joining a bigger force, but now, with Amy in his life, it might be more difficult.

As minutes passed Bill began to feel stupid just standing up on the bridge. Chet wasn't going to come close to it with Bill standing there, plus he had this feeling that Chet was long gone. He could have hitched a ride out of town minutes after they found Claire.

Bill crossed to the far side of the bridge and then walked down into the weeds off to the side of the road. The bugs were buzzing away this time of day. The full sun made his head feel heavy.

Might be smart to tuck himself into the shade under a sprawling oak tree. From there, he could see anyone approaching the bridge from either side. It was a perfect location.

Out of the sun, he was more comfortable, but there was still a warm, sultry wind that blew over the land. The constant movement of the water of the Chippewa hypnotized him. He felt his eyes grow heavy and the sound of buzzing in his ears lulled him to sleep.

In his dream he was running and running after someone, but they were always a few steps ahead of him and they would never turn around so he could get a look at their face and be sure of who they were.

Then something tickled his nose. He brushed it away. Tickled again. His eyes fluttered open and Amy was looking down at him.

"Hard at work?" she asked.

"Holy shit. How did that happen?" He jumped up.

"Don't you know you're never supposed to sit down on the job?"

"Amy, please don't tell anyone. What time is it?"

"You could only have been sleeping a few minutes. Don't worry. I'm sure he didn't sneak by you. Claire told me what she wanted us to do."

"Claire?"

"Yes, remember. Our chief investigator?"

"But I thought she was out of commission."

"Oh, I think she's going to take the rest of the day—a little Vicodin vacation—but I expect to see her at work bright and early tomorrow. She'll want to know that we did what she wanted us to do."

"Heil Claire."

"Hey, don't be nasty, Sleepy. Or should I call you Dopey?"

"So what does she want us to do?"

"Pretty much what you've done, but send someone to Chet's house and tell Rich to be on the lookout."

"Can you do that?" Bill asked.

"Nope, I'm meeting the wife of Mr. Bloaty, or Mrs. Swaggum as she should be known. I'm not looking forward to it. I've never had anyone ID a body before."

"Does she have any idea why he might be down here?"

"I'm not sure. She said this isn't the first time he's disappeared. I got the idea he was kind of a wild man."

Bill said, "Sounds like you could have your hands full."

•   •   •

Meg wasn't sure why her mom had called her for a ride since she knew that Meg couldn't drive yet. Though Meg had just turned sixteen, she still had to take behind-the-wheel lessons and pass the test to get her license. All she could guess was that her mom felt out of it and didn't want to have to arrange anything. Her mom had sounded loopy on the phone so Meg told her not to worry, she'd take care of it. Just to sit tight and someone would come and get her.

First Meg tried to call Bridget. She was pretty sure she wouldn't be home; Meg almost had her aunt's schedule memorized, but she tried there anyway. If she remembered right, she had her regular babysitter today.

Rachel answered the phone and said, "Hello, who is this?" her four-year-old voice sounding soft and high.

"This is your cousin, Meg."

"My Meg?"

"Yes. Is your mom home?"

"Nope. She working."

"Can you tell her I called?"

"Do you want to talk to me now?"

"Rachel, I would love to, but I'm busy."

"I'm busy too. Goodbye." The phone clicked off.

So then Meg decided she would try Curt. She hated to call over to the Hedberg's. His mother always sounded put out when she did. Mrs. Hedberg liked her well enough, but she also thought Meg was corrupting her son.

"Hedberg's residence," a young girl's voice answered.

Oh, good, it was Nelly, Curt's seven-year-old sister. "Hi, Nell. It's Meg. Is Curt around?"

"Nope."

"Where is he?"

"I think he went with Dad to get some stuff from town."

"Do you know when he'll be back?"

"Nope."

Nelly was a nice girl, but not real talkative.

"Could you ask him to call me when he gets home? It's important."

"I'll try."

"Thanks."

Meg hung up the phone and shrugged her shoulders. Hopefully Rich would have his cell phone on. She picked up the phone and dialed the number.

He answered on the third ring. "Hello."

"Hey, Rich. It's Meg."

"What's up?"

"Well, it's Mom. She's fine."

"What's going on? What'd you mean she's fine?"

"She is. It's just she's in the hospital. She broke her arm."

"What? How?"

"I guess she fell, but she's fine. I talked to her." Meg hesitated, then asked, "Do you think you could go and pick her up?

She wants to come home. Says she's too doped up to work."

"Of course. Why didn't she call me?"

"Who knows? She's a little out of it. I think the only number she could remember was home."

"But how did she manage to break her arm? That doesn't sound like her."

"She was chasing someone."

"Figures. Who? Some hardened criminal?"

Meg didn't want to tell him, but knew he would find out sooner or later. Better from her than her mom. "Chet."

CHAPTER 15

Claire sat in a wheelchair waiting. She didn't feel like herself. People were swirling around her in the lobby of the hospital, but she felt very separate from everything: bone distantly throbbing, drifting around in the weird, nauseous pain tempered by the medicine. She grabbed the arms of the wheelchair in order to hold on to something.

Only hours after she picked up Chet, she was back in the lobby of the Chippewa Valley Hospital, except this time she was the patient. It was such a relief that her arm didn't hurt much anymore thanks to the painkillers, but she was sweating like a pig and the perspiration was running into her cast.

Meg had assured her that she'd find someone to pick her up, either Bridget or Curt. If Claire knew her darling daughter, she would probably use this situation to prove that she needed to get her license immediately.

As she sat there, she grew anxious and jittery, wanting to bite someone else's arm or head off. Any extremity would do as long as it made a satisfying snapping sound as it detached. Claire sighed, remembering the slight crack she had heard as she landed on her arm.

The bitch part of herself seemed to be never far away any-more. Ms. Minny Pause, she had come to think of herself.

Suddenly it felt like a hole opened up in the floor and she got sucked down into a vortex of panic: her life was falling apart. Rich had moved out, Chet's wife was horribly dead, her own arm was broken. She was going into menopause and probably had osteoporosis. If there was a bad way to look at something, it presented itself to her at that moment, sitting in a wheelchair in a hospital, all alone.

Long deep breaths, a trick her therapist had taught her years ago to calm panic. Bridget said it would also help with hot flashes. Claire wouldn't mind them so much if they were just flashes but they lasted much longer than that word implied. More like hot hours.

She put a smile on her face, another trick that was supposed to fool the mind into thinking all was well with the world. Just as she looked up, Rich walked through the door and stopped a few feet away from her.

"At least you're smiling," he said, smiling.

"Don't start."

"How is my Claire today?"

"Don't take advantage of me or I'll bash you with my cast." She lifted it up to show him. "Unfortunately these new casts are not quite as good as a weapon as they used to be. They're light and flimsy, but much more comfortable to wear."

"Would you like me to push you out to the car?"

She glanced around. "Since no one's watching, could you take my good arm and let me walk out on my own steam? I hate this wheelchair."

Putting his hands under her arms, he helped her up. She stood for a moment, getting her balance. Whatever drugs they had given her made the world seem foggy and further away, everything smoothed out. Maybe they would help her behave on the ride home. The last thing she wanted to do was yell at Rich again.

"Okay?" he asked.

"Yup. I'm good to go. But let's keep it slow."

They walked out together and Claire again was surprised by how much she needed to lean on him, relying on him for both propulsion and forward momentum. This was not good.

Rich deposited her in the passenger seat, then reached over her to help her strap herself in.

"It's hotter than blazes today," she said.

"It's a warm one." Rich walked around the car, got in, started the engine, and immediately cranked the air-conditioner on high.

Claire leaned her head back and felt the car move forward.

"Do you want to tell me what happened? Meg gave me the bare bones, but you could fill me in."

Claire looked over at Rich. He had kind eyes and lacy wrinkles around them. He was such a good man. What had she ever done to deserve him? Tears leaked out her eyes and down her face.

"Claire?" Rich reached over and patted her knee. "You all right?"

"I'm a mess."

"It's just a broken arm."

"It's not that. It's everything. I let Chet try to hang himself.

Then I let him get away. You don't want to live with me anymore, and Meg wants to have sex. My life is a mess."

"Whoa. Meg wants to have sex?"

"I'm a bad cop. A bad almost-wife. And a bad mom."

Rich laughed. "You are one bad woman all right."

"Not funny." Claire sucked in tears and swallowed.

"There's Kleenex in the glove compartment. Can you tell
me what happened with Chet?"

"Not much to tell. I went to get him at the hospital. Rich,
he looked terrible. I swear. Hunched over in the wheelchair. I
felt so sorry for him. He really suckered me. When we got to the
government center, he took off. I chased after him, almost
caught him, grabbed at him, caught the back of his shirt and
then made the mistake of putting my hand down as I was
falling."

"Ouch."

"It isn't bad enough that our dear friend maybe killed his
wife, but then he has to run away on my watch."

"And you get hurt in the process."

Claire was glad he understood. She went on. "Rich, I think
Chet was trying to kill himself again. When I grabbed him, he
had stepped in front of a truck."

Rich shook his head, didn't say anything.

"Sorry," Claire said.

"Not your fault."

Claire leaned her head back and watched out the window as
the golden fields of late summer rolled by. They were so beautiful: bounty and glory all rolled into one. Claire wished all she
had to do the rest of the day was stare at them, watching them

rolling and undulating under the hot sun. Maybe in a hammock. Maybe with a tall glass of lemonade and a good book. But she still had work to do.

And she feared that what she was seeing was not fields turning gold because it was time, but rather the heat and the drought that accompanied it stressing the crops and drying them out.

She pulled herself up and launched into the speech she had been thinking about since Chet ran away. "Rich, first of all I owe you an apology. I won't even go into how many things I would be apologizing for. Let's just say it's a blanket apology. Second, I'm not sure anymore about Chet. He's almost too perfect as the murderer, but I'm starting to think he didn't kill Anne. Something about the way he was today before he took off. And the ballistics indicate more residue on her hands than his. I guess we're on the same side again."

Rich turned onto Highway 35 going north. Claire felt her eyelids flutter and fall as if weights were attached to them. They'd be home in twenty minutes. She wasn't sure she could stay awake that long.

"We're not on the same side," Rich started, then cleared his throat as if he had something hard to say. "Now I think he did kill her."

•   •   •

Sitting at her desk, Amy called Claire to ask her what to do when Mrs. Swaggum arrived. When Rich answered the phone, he told her that Claire was sleeping. They must have really blasted her with the pain meds. Claire was always on the job. For her to be sleeping with two murder investigations going on was nearly unthinkable.

But what that meant was that Amy was really on her own. Even Bill was out looking for Chet Baldwin. She sat at her desk and tried to think: What questions would Claire ask? The main thing she needed to find out was what Dean's connections were down along the lake. Who did he know? Why would he be down here? Who would want to kill him? Amy figured if she just stayed focused on that, let the conversation go where it might, but always bring it back to the important questions, she would probably do okay.

It wasn't as if this would be her only chance to talk to the wife. Often a trust had to be established before someone would tell them what they needed to know. She had watched Claire do that with victims and perps. Let them talk, listen, ask a question or two—but not so many that they were scared off.

Claire would be back. Soon, Amy hoped.

Jenny, one of the secretaries, told her there was a woman to see her. Amy stood up from her desk, tucked her hair back behind her ears, and walked out to meet Mrs. Swaggum.

The woman was older than Amy expected—she looked to be somewhere in her fifties—and was more nicely dressed than she thought the wife of a tree guy would be. Mrs. Swaggum had on a white linen blouse, a cream-colored skirt, and her blond hair was exploding up high in a spiky hairdo. Big gold hoop earrings and a pale pink lipstick decorated her face. She wore swooping dark sunglasses. A big woman, she carried herself well, like she had a lot to be proud of.

"Thanks for coming all this way," Amy said and then wondered if that was a stupid thing to say. It didn't hurt to be polite.

"You are the deputy?" The woman looked her up and down.

Amy resisted telling Mrs. Swaggum her age and how long she had been a deputy. Instead she just nodded.

"I had to come. I want to see if this is my husband," the woman said, taking her glasses off to reveal large blue eyes, red-rimmed and watery.

"Of course," Amy said and walked around the counter. "If you'll come with me, ma'am. We can take a squad car over to the morgue."

Mrs. Swaggum put her glasses back on. "Please don't ma'am me. Makes me feel old. You can call me Kari."

After they settled in the car, Amy said, "The morgue's in the hospital. It's just a couple blocks away. Won't take but a minute."

"Thank you."

Amy drove as quickly and carefully as she could. She didn't want to ask any questions about Dean Swaggum until she knew for sure that he was the dead man. Even though she was almost a hundred percent sure, it seemed not only insensitive, but very premature. There was a time for such questions and it would be after Kari Swaggum knew her husband was dead.

As they stepped out of the squad car at the hospital, Kari wiped her neck and said, "It's a hot one. I heard this was the tenth day in a row it's been over ninety. That's got to be a record. How do you manage in that uniform?"

"To tell you the truth, I use a lot of deodorant." Amy ushered her toward the entrance.

Kari glanced around. "I've never been here before."

"This hospital?" Amy asked.

"No, this whole area, you know, Durand, Lake Pepin. If I go any place, I always go up to the Cities. It's pretty down here."

"I grew up here," Amy said, then added, "I guess it is pretty."

They were both silent in the elevator going down to the morgue. Amy couldn't help wondering how Kari was feeling, knowing that she might be about to look at her dead husband, yet hoping she wasn't.

When the covered body had been rolled out on the gurney, Amy said, "Let me tell you that the body of this man, whoever he is, has been in the water for a few days. This has made him gain weight, you know, water weight. His face is going to look a little distorted. I just wanted to prepare you for that. Are you ready?"

The older woman nodded, gripping her hands tightly together.

Amy could see the white knuckles on Kari's hands. She pulled back the sheet as gently as she could, only far enough to reveal the man's face. Amy was always impressed with how well the medical examiner fixed the faces after the autopsy, but there was no way to overlook the damage done to this man by the water, the enlarged lips, the pale skin. The poor guy was a mess.

Kari gasped when she saw the bloated face. "Can it possibly be him?"

Amy wasn't going to touch that question.

"I just don't know. I can't believe it's Dean. It doesn't really look like him. He was such a handsome man. May I see the tattoo?" Kari asked.

Amy lowered the sheet so the top of the man's shoulder was showing: Amy had decided that the color of the tattoo was a very dark green, which made sense given it was a tree. The tattoo looked to be about six inches long. The canopy of the tree filled up most of his shoulder muscle with the trunk going down the arm, then the roots spreading out again over his mid-arm.

"Damnation, it has to be him. That stupid tattoo. He was so proud of it. I kept myself from telling him how ridiculous I thought it was. Who puts a tree on their shoulder?" Kari reached out and gently touched the tattoo. "But now it's the only thing left of him that is the same. I wouldn't have even recognized him. What happened? How did he get this way?"

"That's what we're going to find out, and you can help us."

"Please cover him up. I don't want to remember him like this."

Amy pulled the sheet back over his face. Kari doubled over and was silently sobbing, her whole body was shaking as if she was convulsing. This was the piece of dealing with the relatives that she hated, that she didn't know how to handle. A huge part of her wanted to walk around the gurney and hold the weeping woman, but she had learned, watching Claire, that it was more respectful to let them have their moment of grief. Just stand by and be a witness to it without saying anything.

Amy was afraid that the woman was going to fall over so she walked behind her and found a chair and brought it to her. Kari sat down and slowly unbent, wiping her face and shuddering. "Thank you."

"Can I get you a glass of water?"

"I need to get out of here first. Is there somewhere we can go?"

Amy thought fast. It was so hot outside that she couldn't suggest that. Then she remembered there was a cafeteria in the hospital. She didn't want to bring the woman back to the sheriff's department. Keep it more intimate.

Once they both ordered coffee and sat down at a table, Amy said, "First let me say how sorry I am for your husband's death. It must be a real shock."

Kari lifted her head and gave Amy a tight smile. "You have no idea."

"May I ask you a few questions? Are you up to it?"

"I'd rather not have to come down here again so yes, ask away."

"Kari, how long has your husband been gone? When did you last see him?"

Kari thought for a second, then said, "It will be a week tonight. The longest he's ever been gone. I have to admit I was starting to get worried. I made a few phone calls, checking with friends, guys who hung out with him, even customers. But I tried not to think about it too much. It's just the way Dean was."

"What do you mean?"

"Oh, he'd need a little adventure from time to time. It wasn't a big deal to me. I mean, I was his wife. I knew what he was like when I married him."

"What do you mean by adventure?"

"Oh, various things. A road trip. A hunting trip. Maybe a poker game that went on for a few days."

"So he would go off from time to time?"

"Yes. You know I'm older than he was and we had dated for a while before we married. I knew what I was getting into. He needed me. I always knew that. I always knew he would come back." Her voice broke, but she continued, "Except now he won't."

"What was he doing on this side of the river?"

"Oh, he took jobs over here from time to time. He liked working along the river. People would hire him for these big cutting jobs. Sometimes I'd go watch him. He was amazing. He would climb up to the very top of a tree and then slowly take it down. A real artist. He loved his work."

"Was he working for someone in particular?"

"Not that I know of. I didn't have that much to do with the business. He managed it on his own. I have my own money. My last husband left me well off, so I let Dean do what he wanted. He loved being outside. It kept him healthy. Kept him from drinking too much. I think it kept him alive, until it didn't."

Kari stopped talking for a moment, then blurted out, "How did he die?"

Amy was surprised that she hadn't told the woman that yet. "Sorry. I thought I told you. He was shot."

"Where?"

"In the belly."

Kari's hands flew up to her face. "Oh my god. Tell me he didn't live long."

Amy swallowed and did as Kari wanted. "He would have died very quickly." She had no idea if this was true.

"Kari, I need you to think and tell me if there was anyone who might have wanted to hurt him."

Kari gave Amy a look.

Amy was more specific. "You know, is there anyone you can think of who might have wanted him dead?"

"I can't imagine. Dean was a really nice guy. I mean, he never did anything mean. He just liked everybody and sometimes that got him in trouble."

"How so?"

Kari lifted her chin, pushed her hair back from her face, and said, "Well, he never met a woman he didn't like."

•   •   •

"Where have you been?" Rich asked when Meg walked in the door after eleven o'clock. Hard to tell, because she was just wearing shorts and a t-shirt, but she looked a little rumpled to him. He wondered what she had been up to. "I thought you'd stick around. You disappeared on me when I was getting your mom situated upstairs."

"Sorry. I thought I told you. Curt and I had plans to go to a movie that was going to close after tonight. I knew you could take care of Mom better than me," she said as she pushed her hair back from her face.

"Hey, speaking of you and Curt, your mom tells me you two are getting kinda steamy."

"What does that mean? Kinda steamy?"

Rich wished he wouldn't have brought it up. But he was as much of a dad as Meg would ever have. He plowed on. "You know, getting intimate."

"Geez, why did she have to tell you that?"

"Why shouldn't she?"

"Well, it was a private conversation between the two of us, that's why. Why is my sex life an open book when I don't bug you guys about yours?"

"Don't think it's the same thing. We're old hands at it." Then he thought about Claire worrying that she might be pregnant. Maybe it was the same thing.

"Gross." Meg sat down at the counter and asked, "Well, since you brought it up—how old were you when you had sex for the first time?"

Rich thought back to Susy Parker in the back seat of his mom's station wagon. "Can't remember back that far."

"Right." Meg laughed. "I believe that. Mom sleeping?"

Rich waved his hand toward the upstairs. "Yeah, she went to bed about three hours ago. She's pretty tanked on painkillers. I got her to eat something, then put her to bed. She's actually pretty cute when she gets high."

"She going to be okay?"

"I think she'll be fine soon. And probably cranky as anything. It's frustrating having only one good arm. She won't like it."

"Can't imagine." Meg looked at Rich. "I've never broken anything so far in my life. Have you?"

"Broke my leg when I was twenty riding a cow. Stupidest thing I ever did. The cow didn't like it either. It started running and I slid off the tail end and landed wrong on my left leg. Impossible to drive a stick shift with a broken leg."

"You're staying here tonight, aren't you?"

"Yeah, I think I better. I have a feeling your mom needs me."

Meg snorted, then laughed. "Duh, Rich. Like she always does."

CHAPTER 16

When Claire woke up in the morning, she felt like she had had the best night's sleep in ages. The sun was pouring through the window, higher in the sky than she was used to seeing it from bed. What time was it?

Then she tried to move and almost clubbed herself with her cast. Her arm ached, her shoulder felt like it had come unhinged. She needed a pain pill, but not the amount she had taken yesterday. She couldn't continue to be as snowed under by the pain meds as she was yesterday, not if she wanted to get any work done.

Claire clutched her cast to her chest and tried to roll gently off the bed, without jarring anything. Her feet found the floor and she stood up, then fell back on the bed. Her head was reeling.

"You up?" Rich shouted from downstairs.

"I think so."

"You need some help?"

Claire looked down at what she was wearing. Somehow Rich had taken her uniform off of her last night and tied a bathrobe around her to wear to bed. She didn't think she could get dressed by herself. "I'm afraid so."

Rich walked into the room and asked, "I think putting a bra on is going to be difficult. Do you need to wear one today?"

"I think I better."

"It might be painful."

"I know. Just be gentle."

Rich brought her a bra. "This one okay?"

"As good as any."

First he eased the broken arm under the strap, then she slipped the other one in, then he pulled it tight around her back and started to fasten it.

She smiled at him. "You did it perfectly."

"I'm better at taking them off," he said.

"Ha-ha."

"Oh, your sense of humor has returned." He went into her drawer and found a large short-sleeved shirt. Again, they started with him managing the broken limb.

After the shirt was on, he rummaged through her drawers and threw her a pair of underpants, which she caught with one hand.

"See if you can get those on by yourself."

After no insignificant effort, she got them around her feet. "What are you, some kind of sadist? Help."

"Stand up," he ordered, then pulled the underpants up.

In her top drawer, he found a pair of baggy pants that had elastic at the top. Together they managed to pull those on, then Claire flopped back down on the bed and said, "I'm exhausted."

"It's after ten o'clock."

"No way."

"If you don't get some coffee into your system soon, you'll probably go into severe withdrawal. I've got a pot waiting for you downstairs."

Claire stood up slowly. Rich was watching her. "I'm fine," she said as she took her first steps across the room.

"I'm right here." He put an arm under her shoulder. "You need to take it easy today."

"I don't think I'm up to driving today so I was wondering if you could take me over to Chet's."

"Claire, I talked to the sheriff. He said he didn't want to see your face down there today. Can't you just take a day off?"

Even though the urge to snap back at him was strong, Claire held it in. "I know that I should crawl back in bed and rest. I know that. You don't need to tell me." A little crankiness leaked out there so she reined it in. "Sorry. I mean I get it. And I will crawl back in bed. But when we were at Chet's I didn't get all their personal papers. At the time I didn't think I needed them. But now I feel like there's something I'm not getting about what happened over there. I want to try to understand what was going on in their lives. They were my friends too, Rich. I want to figure this out. If you would just take me over there for a few minutes, that's all I'd need."

"Promise you'll come back here and take it easy?" he asked.

"Yes, I absolutely promise."

On the ride over, they were both quiet in the car. Claire was surprised how the pain meds emptied her mind of trivialities. She had taken a half dose, which meant she could still feel the ache of her arm, but she could also see the world outside the car window, the pattern of the trees moving through the forest, the sumac showing a tinge of their fall color in the tips of their leaves, the heat making her drowsy and content. It wasn't unpleasant, this slightly drugged feeling. In an odd way, it made some things clearer, what was really important in life stood out in stark relief against all the petty things she worried about.

Claire turned and looked at Rich. He was more solid than the bluffs. "Please don't stay over there anymore."

"What?"

"I don't want you to stay at Chet's."

"But I thought you wanted me there in case he came home."

"It's not that important. I want you with me."

He slid his hand over and stroked the tip of her fingers that stuck out of the end of her cast. "You got it."

• • •

Bentley and Rich had definitely come to an understanding about how a dog should behave. The dog walked out to meet the car. No jumping up, which was good. It meant Rich didn't have to worry that Bentley might jump up on Claire. Once Rich ushered Claire into the house, he went to take care of the rest of the chores.

Bentley followed him around the farm, helping him let the horses out to pasture, watching as he made sure there was enough water for them on these hot days. He observed with intense interest Rich filling his food bowl, but didn't touch it until Rich said he could. While the dog ate, Rich mucked out the horses' stalls, not his favorite job. Then the two of them walked out to the garden together. Cucumbers, green beans, zucchini were ripening faster than he could pick them.

Rich picked some tomatoes that were so ripe they were almost splitting. They filled his hand with their deep redness. He couldn't resist—he bit into one and the sweet juice ran down his chin. He swore there was nothing as good as a fresh-picked, sunbursting tomato.

But the red juice reminded him, unfortunately, of the recent scene in the house.

"Bentley, what the hell happened here? Who killed Anne?"

The dog perked up his ears and wagged his tail, but said nothing.

"He said you went for a walk with him that night. I wish you could talk, you old mutt."

Bentley pulled back his lips in an odd mimic of a grin. Rich reached down and ruffled his fur. "You're a good dog. You keep an eye out for your master. He might be heading this way."

Then Rich went to the cabin and gathered up his gear.

When he walked into Chet's house to see how Claire was doing, it was the first time he had been inside since the night Anne died. It smelled stale and he wondered if he should come back and empty out the refrigerator. They had left the airconditioning set fairly high so it wasn't too hot in the house, but it just felt all closed up.

Claire was digging through some drawers in the kitchen under the counter.

"How're you doing? I'm all done with the animals."

"I think I've got most of what I need. Anne's purse, their checkbooks, most recent bills." She looked down at the box she had filled with papers. "No one took any of this yesterday because we were waiting to talk to Chet. I kept thinking I'd get over here. If I could have talked to him, I might not need to be digging through his life."

"Don't you need a search warrant for that stuff?"

"Not for a crime scene."

"You find anything?"

"I don't know yet, but I'm about ready to go."

"Hey, I have something I think you need to know about." He held up a baggy.

"What's in there?"

"A condom."

"Where'd you find it?"

"In the cabin." He hesitated. "I know Anne was on birth control. Chet mentioned it once in passing. They didn't want to have kids. So he didn't need to use a condom when he was with her."

Claire took the baggy and stared at the item. "And you're sure this belongs to Chet?"

•   •   •

Chet had spent the night in an old hunting cabin. His friend who owned the place came down from Chicago once or twice a year and used the cabin for deer hunting. The key was over the door jamb. No reason for any real security, nothing much to steal. More critters inside the house than out, but they didn't bother him.

When he got up in the morning he found a box of old saltine crackers with not much crunch left to them, but the salt and flour mixed in his mouth and made his stomach feel not so empty. He got some water out of the old cistern, hoped it wouldn't give him any bad disease. But not a big concern since he wasn't planning on being around that long.

He was doing penance. He hadn't run away from Claire to free himself; he had run so that he would have a moment to think and remember who he was. Before everything had gone wrong. So very wrong.

His clothes, which had been wet from the river, were bone-dry in the heat of the day. It had taken Chet a long time to fall asleep. Finally he had dropped off in the early morning quiet, right before sunrise, and hadn't woken up until past mid-day. The heat was coming on strong, he needed to move. Another good reason to keep to the trees when he continued his walk.

He knew where he was going. He was going home.

Chet had never walked to the cabin from his farm but he figured it was probably about eight miles as the crow flies and since he would be trying to keep to the woods, it would probably take him a good four to five hours. He'd get there just about sundown.

The woods were thick this time of year. Too hot for ticks but the flies buzzed the back of his neck as he walked through the understory of the forest. The gooseberries were green, not ready to pick yet, but the black caps were plentiful and he stopped when he saw a good batch and picked a handful or two.

As he walked he went over his path in his mind: he could take Bear Pen Road over to D, then cut through the woods to Porcupine Lane. Stick near Elk Creek Road, then catch up to Goat Back. That would take him right close to home: Baldwin

Lane. His own road and everything. Anne had loved that he had a road named after him. At first, it had been so easy to please her.

He had hunted around his property and knew all the deer paths and farm roads that he could use to avoid walking on the main roads, not that they even got much traffic back up on the bluffs.

He wondered what he was walking into, if the cops would be there waiting for him. He'd have to take that chance. For the last time in his life, he was walking as a free man in the world, eating berries, feeling sweat pour down the back of his neck. Everything he had always taken for granted.

But then that's what started all this. Something he had always taken for granted. They say you never know what you got 'til it's gone and couldn't be truer words said, or sung for that matter.

He felt his neck. Still sore from his attempt to leave the world. Dumb thing to do, but, at the time, seemed like the only option.

He remembered a fairy tale he had loved as a kid: This guy goes fishing and catches a magic fish who can grant him three wishes. The guy is all happy but he makes the big mistake of letting his selfish wife in on the deal. She just wants bigger and bigger palaces until they all come crumbling down and then he and his wife are both back, happy to be in their own little house and he goes fishing again. Or something like that.

If he had one wish, all he would want is to see Anne leaning over the kitchen sink again, washing up some dishes, her hands all soapy, turning to look at him as he walked in the door. Kiss-

ing him, touching him with her soapy hands, saying, You are forgiven, you are forgiven.

Not possible, so there was only one thing left for him to do.

CHAPTER 17

Claire found there was no way she could stay in bed and work on the Baldwin papers. It was a nice idea, but completely uncomfortable. The bills and records kept sliding off the bedcovers; she couldn't keep track of anything. Plus it made her arm hurt even more.

Making a couple trips, she carted everything back downstairs and set herself up at the kitchen table. She was able to rest her arm on the table and take the weight off her shoulder. Much better. She used a couple of small cast-iron frying pans to prop various items open: the Baldwin's three checkbooks—his, hers, and theirs—the calendars, the telephone books.

She had decided to go back over the last year and comb through all the bills, the receipts, every document. After that she would try to get on the Baldwin's computer and check their email. She would have to call on either Bill or Jeremy to do that. They were the resident experts.

But first the checkbooks. She decided to start with Anne's. Claire liked reading through checkbooks. The entries told the story of someone's life—where they shopped for food, how often they serviced their car, what they spent their money on. From the handwriting alone, delicate and crisp, Claire would have guessed that this was Anne's checkbook. From the entries, she saw that Anne paid the household bills: Schaul gas, Century-Tel, Xcel energy.

Anne shopped at Paul and Fran's in Pepin, with occasional splurges at the Nelson Cheese Factory and the Smiling Pelican bakery. She dropped a bundle up at DSW in the cities on shoes in April. About once a month, there would be a check made out to the Harbor View Cafe; they were regular customers—no surprise there. And she supported the wonderful art and craft shops in the area.

In mid-June there was a check made out to a Dr. Singh. Probably just a regular check-up, but worth looking into. Then Claire noticed that every subsequent week there was another check made out to Dr. Singh. So these were not physical check-ups. Possibly mental health or a chiropractor. Very worth looking into.

By July, Claire was taking her time. The regular checks for groceries and gas she ignored, but there was a check made out to Timber Services. She would call them up and see what it was about.

The last check was made out to the liquor store in Red Wing. She wondered if Chet and Anne had enjoyed their last drinks together. Sad.

The credit card bills showed much the same pattern of shopping. Nothing jumped out at her: gas, The Best of Times bookstore, supplies at the Cenex, the post office.

Putting aside the bills and checks, Claire pulled out a box containing the contents of their medicine cabinet, and the pills she found next to the refrigerator. Again, what you might expect to find: aspirin, Sudafed, Vitamin C, calcium. But there were five pharmacy bottles containing prescription drugs: Lexapro, Lipitor, Flomax, finestreride, and Viagra.

Viagra for Chet. That surprised her a bit. Chet always struck her as brimming with testosterone. But he was in his mid-fifties, about fifteen years older than Anne. Lexapro she knew was an antidepressant, that prescription was for Anne. Lipitor for Chet's high cholesterol. But the other two she wasn't familiar with. She'd have to ask Bridget.

She wanted to see if she could find Anne's Dr. Singh so she got out the phone book. She'd try Red Wing first. There were few doctors on their side of the river—most of the local clinics and hospitals were in Minnesota. Claire lucked out. There was one listing for a Dr. Singh and after the phone number it read: "Family counseling, chemical dependency counseling, and panic and anxiety." Claire would have to get a court order and see what the good doctor might reveal.

• • •

"How do you know where this place is?" Amy asked Bill as he turned down a dirt road heading into the woods.

"The sheriff told me. He said it was owned by a friend of Chet's, thought it'd be worth a look-see."

"Can't believe how blasted hot it is. When are we going to get a break?" Amy rested her head back on the seat and looked out the window at the large oaks shading the road. "It feels a bit cooler here in the trees."

"Yeah, I'm sure ready for this hot spell to break. I think I'm getting a rash on my behind."

"Oh, how romantic. You'll have to show me."

"My pleasure," he smiled.

Bill could never drive slowly, even down a dirt road, maybe especially down a dirt road. When they came in sight of the cabin, he slammed on the brakes and dust flew up all around them.

"Our own private dust storm," Amy said quietly.

"Huh?" Bill asked.

The cabin looked as if it was slowly sinking into the ground. Amy got out of the car and walked up to the front door. The wooden door was cracked, only a few peelings of paint protected it. She tried the door, but found it locked. She walked around and looked in a window, but couldn't see much of anything. When she yanked the window, it flew up.

"Hey, Bill, I'm going in."

He looked over at her, but didn't make a move in her direction. "Go for it. Think I'll wait for you to unlock the door."

After squeezing through the window opening, she landed on the floor in a heap. Dust stirred up and she sneezed. The one-room cabin was dark and cool, an old card table with two chairs took up the middle of the room with two bunk beds built into a far corner.

Amy heard a gentle rapping on the door. "I'm coming," she said and picked herself up off the floor.

After fumbling with the old lock, she finally turned it the right way and the door opened. "How was your day, darling?" she asked.

"Fine, lover." Bill walked in, leaned over her and planted a kiss on her upturned face.

The first kiss was a quick peck on the cheek, appropriate for "Father Knows Best," but then he moved to her lips.

Amy pushed him away and said, "Not during work."

Bill pulled her close and whispered in her ear, "But we're not at work, we're home. Come on." He grabbed her tightly around the waist and started to rub against her.

She made herself turn to wood. "Stop it."

Instead of stopping, Bill slid his hands up under her shirt.

She tried to push him away, but he grabbed her shirt and was lifting it over her head. "Not now," she said, her voice muffled in fabric. At the sound of her voice, he stopped, left her shirt turned inside-out over her face and arms. His hands slid down her body.

As Bill's hands undid her pants, Amy started to get frantic. He wasn't stopping. Her arms were trapped in her shirt. She couldn't breath with her face covered with the shirt. She kicked out at him and slammed her head into his chest.

"Ooh, I like it like that," Bill said. "A little wild."

The shirt fell down far enough for her face to be uncovered and Amy screamed as loud as she could.

Bill stopped and looked at her. "What?"

She took a deep breath, then spit out each word, carefully and separately, "I — don't — want — to — do — this."

He looked a bit embarrassed, ran his hand over his mouth and joked, "What? Just thought we'd have a little fun."

Amy yanked her shirt down and stared at him. "This is not fun. Not for me. What's the matter with you? Some kind of pervert?"

"What's the matter with you?" Bill threw up his hands, but

stepped back from her. "You're acting like we haven't done this before? Like I'm trying to rape you or something?"

"Whenever a man forces himself on a woman it's rape."

"What? Rape 101. Are you serious? Come on, Ame. What's wrong with getting it on? We're not doing anything wrong."

"I told you not during work. I told you that. What do you not understand about that?"

"Okay. Enough already. I get it." Bill stood in the doorway. "I didn't know you were such a prude."

Amy felt like her hair was going to fly off her head. "I'm not a prude. I just don't want to have sex while I'm working in a dirty, dusty cabin."

Bill stayed in the doorway, but turned his back to her.

Let him be mad, she thought. She smoothed her hair back from her face and tried to gather her wits about her, as her mom would say.

Amy examined the cabin, walking around and looking at the floor. It was hard to tell but she thought she saw footprints. But who knows when someone had last been in the place.

At first she would have said that no one had been there recently, but then she noticed a package of crackers open on the table.

"Crackers," she said and sat down at the table. "Looks like someone opened these recently."

"You talking to me?" Bill turned and asked, sarcastically. Then added, "How do you figure?"

"Mice. There's no way this place isn't crawling with them and they would have demolished these crackers before now."

"Good work, detective. So we know someone has been here recently. So what does that prove?"

Amy picked up a cracker and broke it in half. It was soggy. "Well, actually we know more than that. We know that someone who was famished was here recently. No one else would have bothered with these crackers."

"So there's a chance that Chet was here."

"Yes, which would mean that he's on this side of the river and probably heading east. Which would support what Claire said—that he was probably going home."

•   •   •

Bridget tied her hair back, splashed her face with ice water, and wafted her arms up and down. She had to talk to Claire about putting air-conditioning into this house of hers. She had been renting it for a few years, but they hadn't had a hot summer like this one for a long time.

"Come on, Rachel. Going to Auntie Claire's, Uncle Rich's and Meg's."

"My Meg?"

"Yes." For some reason, Rachel insisted that Meg was hers. Meg was more like an older sister than a cousin to four-year-old Rachel.

When Bridget turned around, she saw that her darling daughter had decided to take off all her clothes. "What happened to your shirt and shorts?"

"Don't like 'em."

"Well, this isn't up for debate." Bridget found the pile of clothes in the hallway outside the bathroom and proceeded to pull the light t-shirt over her daughter's head.

"Don't like it." Rachel flung her arms around.

"Not even your cute donkey?" Bridget pointed to the picture of Eeyore on the front of the t-shirt.

"Don't want it." Rachel tried to take it off.

"You have to wear clothes to go see Meg. She wants to see your donkey."

"See the donkey?" Rachel asked.

"Yup," Bridget quickly pulled on the shorts. "Let's get in the car, baby. It'll be cooler in there."

After the two minute ride over, during which the air-conditioning did nothing to cool down the car, walking into Rich's house felt like walking into a freezer. Bridget had the urge to lay down on the floor and soak up the cool.

Claire came walking out of the kitchen and Meg came bounding down the stairs. Rachel squealed with delight.

"I'll take her up to my room," Meg said, hoisting Rachel up to her hip and carting her off.

"Thanks," Bridget said.

Claire held up her arm.

"I see. How broken is it?"

"Asked like a true doctor. Badly. The bone snapped, then shifted. They had to set it. Torture of the worst kind. The doctor said a good two months."

"At least it's your left arm."

"There is a reason we have two arms."

Bridget could tell her sister was on the edge. "How's the menopause going?"

"Sweating like a pig, but with this weather, everyone is."

Bridget knew that estrogen had become a dirty word with many women, who because of some recent studies, feared the long-term effects. "You could go on a low-dose of estrogen just to get you through the transition. Take it for a year or so and that might ease you through."

"Ease me through to what—permanent cronedom?" Claire squinched her nose. "I'll think about it."

Letting that subject drop, Bridget sat down at the kitchen table and looked at the piles of paper and the line-up of pill bottles. "Are you organizing your life, Claire?"

"Not mine. I'm just trying to figure out what it all is. It's Chet and Anne's. What's left of it."

"How sad. Do you know what happened yet?"

"Not really. They still haven't found Chet. Every hour he's missing I'm afraid he'll be found dead."

"So you think he killed Anne?"

"I did. I was sure at first. Now I just don't know what to think." Claire pushed over the pill bottles. "What can you tell me about these?"

Bridget picked up the closest one, Lexapro, and read the label. "Very common anti-depressant, anti-anxiety. Low dose. Probably trying to nip it in the bud."

"The Lexapro's for Anne. I have to say I'm surprised to know she was on an antidepressant."

"Totally common these days. You can't believe how many

prescriptions I fill a day."

"These four are for Chet."

"Well, Lipitor. You know that. Just for cholesterol. Very common for a man his age." Then Bridget scanned the remaining three bottles. "Hmm. Looks like he was having some prostate problems. Fairly serious problems. Had he had surgery?"

"Not that he told us. But I'm thinking the two of them were keeping some secrets. I'll ask Rich if he knows."

"Well, from the looks of these meds, I'd guess that your friend Chet was having trouble being sexually active. Viagra might have helped, but not necessarily. Not if he had had the surgery."

"Thanks," Claire said. "So he can't get it up and she's on an antidepressant. Not exactly the happy couple we had imagined."

CHAPTER 18

Dr. Singh?" Claire asked the gentle voice that had answered the phone.

"Yes, this is she."

"My name is Claire Watkins. I'm calling from the Pepin County Sheriff's department. Was Anne Baldwin a patient of yours?" She tucked the phone under her chin and tapped her pencil on the pad of paper she had ready to take notes. With one hand it was difficult.

"I don't talk about who my patients are. Why are you calling me?"

"I'm sorry. I don't mean to get off on the wrong foot with you, Dr. Singh. I already know that Anne was your patient. I would like to ask you some questions, if you have a moment." Claire didn't quite know how to phrase her next question. "Have you heard what has happened to her?"

"Anne? Something has happened to her?"

"Yes, I'm sorry to tell you this, but Anne has died."

A gasp. "No. What happened?"

"We're not sure exactly what happened, but it appears Anne died of a gunshot wound to the head three days ago in her home."

"This is so terrible. Was it an accident?"

"We're not sure. That's why I'm calling you. I'm wondering if I could come and talk to you about her."

Long pause. "How did you know she was my client?"

"I looked through her bills and saw that she was seeing you. We're trying to understand if she might have been in the state of mind where she would have shot herself."

"This is very difficult. I don't feel that I can talk about Anne. Client confidentiality."

"I understand that you must protect the privacy of your clients. But technically, is that necessary anymore? She's dead."

"Anne's death is a great loss, but it does not effect the agreement that I make with all my clients when we begin a course of therapy. You understand."

Her last sentence was not a question. Claire hoped they could work this out together and she wouldn't be forced to go to a judge. "According to what I know from the Wisconsin State Psych Board, if you felt that she was a danger either to herself or to others, you, as her therapist, should have made that known to the proper authorities. Now there is a very good chance that she killed herself. Let me ask you this—did you ever consider contacting the police because of her state of mind? Were you ever concerned for her safety?"

"These are difficult questions."

"Why? Why are they difficult questions? You must face them all the time." Claire could hear her own voice rising. She drew a peace sign on the piece of paper to remind herself to stay calm. It would do no good, she was sure, getting belligerent with this woman. "Did you consider her mental health a risk in any way? Did you ever think she might kill herself?"

"I'm afraid I can say no more."

Claire could hear the woman was shutting down on her. "I need this information. If you won't give it to me, I'll have to go to a judge."

"That is your prerogative."

Claire calculated how long that might take. "If I get a court order, might I come and speak with you tomorrow afternoon?"

Rustling of papers. "I would be free after five. If you bring a court order, I might consent to a conversation."

"Thank you, Dr. Singh. I hope to see you tomorrow." Claire looked at the peace sign again. Give the woman something. "I'm sorry about the loss of your patient." She couldn't help adding, "She was a friend of mine."

"Yes, this is a very sad day."

•   •   •

Even though they had parked in the shade, the back of the car was getting steamy. Meg sat sprawled over Curt, her legs in his lap, his arms around her waist. They had been kissing so long that her lips buzzed.

Curt strapped his big watch to Meg's small wrist. They both laughed at how ridiculous it looked.

He said, "I should go in about five minutes. The cows don't like to wait. You're in charge. You keep track of the time."

Meg slipped the watch off her wrist and handed it back to

him. "I have to get home too. My mom is having kind of a hard time with her broken arm and all."

"Listen," Curt said as he slid his hands back around her waist. "My folks are going away this weekend. They're going to some farm auction. I have to stay home and milk the cows."

"You and those cows." Meg looked down at his hands. "That's why you're so good at all this making out and such."

For a second Curt looked like he had swallowed his tongue.

Meg laughed. He loved to mess around, but he didn't like to talk about it. Curt was a good talker, thinking of being a philosopher, but he got embarrassed whenever she brought up the subject of sex.

"So what're you saying?" she asked.

"I don't know. I thought maybe you'd like to come over for a picnic. I could make some hamburgers or something."

"Just the two of us?"

"Yeah, my sister's going with them."

"We'll be all alone?"

"Yeah. That's the point, isn't it?"

"The point of what?"

He pulled his hands away and sat up. Squished into the back of his Ford Escort made it difficult for either of them to move. "Do I have to spell it out?"

"Yes," she said.

"S-E-X."

"It's all sex, Curt. Everything. Kissing, touching. Not any one act is considered sex."

"This is driving me crazy, Meg."

"That's because we don't talk about it and decide what we both want to do and what would be best for us to do right now when we're only sixteen and living with our parents."

"Okay, do you want to sleep with me? Go all the way? Run to home base? Pop the cherry? Is that clear enough?"

"Yes, but not very romantic."

"I don't think being squished in the back of this car is very romantic."

Since Curt was a good half a foot taller than her, Meg guessed he was a lot more uncomfortable at this moment than she was.

"Do you?" he asked again.

"I don't know. It just seems so big."

• • •

Night was falling over his meadow. Standing at the edge of the field, Chet Baldwin could see that his horses had been put away. He didn't see Rich's truck in the driveway so he assumed he wasn't still around.

It was a time of day in summer that Chet felt he could never get enough of. The brilliant heat of the afternoon had dropped out of the air and left an embracing warmth along with the muted colors of the inside of a flower hanging in the sky.

Seeing the sky that way reminded him of Anne. He could hear her voice in his head. She had taught him how to see the world. Not just see it but enjoy it. Life with her had been such a pleasure. Not that they hadn't had their troubles, especially lately, but more and more the richness of their life together was coming back to him. What would she want him to do now? He kept asking himself that. If Anne were here, what would she tell him to do?

Staying in the deep shadows of the treeline, Chet walked through the tall grass at the edge of the field. One thing he knew for sure—he wanted to be home. He would run no more. Whatever would happen would happen on the farm.

The other thing he was sure of was he needed a drink. Big boulders of memory crashed around in his head that he could not bear. He was hoping if he drank enough liquor they would stop. He couldn't stand to think of what had happened in the last couple weeks. It ripped him in two. It made him want to hurt something. Hurt himself again.

As he got close to the house, he had a new worry. Wouldn't the sheriff and Claire know he'd come back here? Wouldn't they be waiting for him? There was no car in the driveway, but they could have parked far away and walked in.

He crouched under a tree at the edge of the yard, just past the garden, and waited. If anyone was in the house they would turn some lights on soon.

He stayed in a squat, quite sure he couldn't be seen from the house. Darkness was creeping over the land, its soft black hand scooping up all the stray light remaining in the sky.

If he could only turn back time to three weeks ago.

He and Anne would be sitting out on the back patio, swatting the occasional mosquito, laughing, talking about the weather, the crops, what the fall would bring—if it would ever come. Touching hands as they handed each other a drink, some chips, just to know the other was there in the gathering dark.

He wondered where she was now. If he would see her again. If it would be very soon.

Just then he felt a touch on his shoulder. A slobbery tongue reached out and licked his face.

CHAPTER 19

As Amy stood on the doorstep of a rambler in Hastings, she hoped Mrs. Swaggum would let her look through Dean's files. She pushed back her shoulder-length blond hair. She wished she had a band to put it into a ponytail and get it off her neck.

Amy didn't think she'd need a search warrant—after all, she was investigating the murder of the woman's husband—and she was praying Mrs. Swaggum wouldn't send her packing. The hour drive back to Durand would mean she would have to come back another day.

It was still beastly hot out, but the weatherman promised a break in the weather, maybe even a thunderstorm by tonight.

When Mrs. Swaggum opened the door, Amy was surprised to see how changed she looked. The older woman was wearing no make-up and her hair was in a tangle, which aged her a good ten years.

"Mrs. Swaggum, we had talked about me going through your husband's office. I tried to call earlier but the line kept being busy."

"I put the phone off the hook." A hand drifted up to her ratted and uncombed hair.

"May I come in?" Amy asked.

Mrs. Swaggum stepped back and Amy entered a clean living room. "Come this way. The office is off the garage. Stay as long as you like."

Swaggum's place of business overflowed with paper, empty Mountain Dew cans and newspapers. There was no glimpse of the desk that must have been holding all that clutter up. Duct tape bandaged the seat of the desk chair, which was the only place to sit. The shades hung off the window like the carcasses of some old birds. Dust covered every surface with a felt finish.

A huge impulse to turn and run flooded Amy, but then she saw a small air-conditioning unit, turned it on, and got comfortable in the duct-taped seat, which was surprisingly comfortable. The hum of the unit filled the room with white noise. A cool breeze settled on her shoulders. No people talking at her, the room became a little womb of cool. She wouldn't mind staying for an hour or two. She might even find something.

While she wasn't particularly neat herself, Amy liked order. Her desk at work was arranged so she knew where everything was. She cleared off a section of Swaggum's desk, temporarily piling those papers on the floor.

She was stunned to see bills from seven years ago still floating in the paper sea. Anything over two years old, she stuffed in a cardboard box she found in the garage. Using her own judgment she just figured it would be hard to hold a grudge for that long.

Hours later she had sorted all the papers by year and had read through everything from two years ago. As she started into the current year, she felt her stomach rumble. She was starving. She stuffed all the current bills and papers in the box to take back to the office.

Mrs. Swaggum came to the door. She looked at the desk and then around the cleared room. "We should have hired you."

Amy showed her what she had done with the various boxes. "Is it all right if I take these with me? I'll return them."

"Hey, I'd just have to go through them myself. If you find any outstanding client bills, let me know. I didn't pay attention to Dean's work. Even though it was a mess in here, he seemed to manage. I think he kept it all in his head." Mrs. Swaggum's face crumpled. "I miss him so much already. He was my buddy."

The word "buddy" jolted Amy in the heart. That described how she felt about Bill. Amy stood with the box of paper in her arms and watched Mrs. Swaggum try to pull her face back into shape. She knew she needed to say something.

"We'll find out who did this to him," Amy said.

Mrs. Swaggum patted her face, blinking her eyes to clear the tears. "I don't really care. I mean, I know it's your job. But it won't bring him back. It'll never bring him back."

Amy carted the box of bills and papers out to the squad car and slid it into the back seat. As she shoved the box to secure it, some of the papers came spilling over the top. She reached down and gathered them up. An invoice caught her eye, so she unfolded it:

June 28

Please pay Timber Tree Service $800.00 for services rendered.

The name of the customer was Chet Baldwin.

•   •   •

"You're going to work today?" Rich asked as he got out of the pickup truck and saw Claire sitting on the deck, dressed in her uniform.

Claire could hear by his tone of voice that he didn't think it was a good idea. "I'll take it easy. Amy is picking me up. With these two murder cases, I just don't feel I can take much time off."

"You could."

Claire decided not to argue with Rich. Even though he had stayed at the house last night, he had slept down on the couch, supposedly so she could get some sleep and not worry about hitting him with her cast, but there was definitely some mending that needed to happen between them. She wanted him back in their bed.

"Everything look okay over at Baldwin's?" Claire asked. "No sign of Chet?" She had told the sheriff that she and Rich would keep an eye out for the missing man. They didn't have the manpower to keep a deputy stationed over there.

"Nope. Didn't notice anything out of the ordinary. You think Chet would really go back there?"

"What do you think?" Claire asked. "You know him better than almost anyone."

"That's what I thought, but now I don't feel like I know him at all." Rich pulled his t-shirt out from his body and blew down the front of it. "It wouldn't surprise me if he showed up."

"The sheriff said he'll have the deputies do drive-bys. You be careful if you go over there," Claire said.

"I'm not worried. Chet wouldn't do anything to me."

"How do you know?"

Rich walked into the house without answering.

Amy drove up in the squad car and Claire headed to the passenger side, which felt odd to her. She was usually the driver.

It surprised Claire how awkward every action was because of her broken arm. It was even difficult getting into the squad car. She ungracefully landed on the passenger seat holding her cast against her body and said hi.

Amy started talking so fast about papers that had slid out of a box and what she had found in Hastings that Claire had to hold up her good hand and stop her.

"Start over. Pretend I've had a serious brain injury and you have to be very slow and clear with me."

"Are you still on meds?" Amy asked.

"No. But I feel like there's residuals in my system, and my arm …"

"It still hurts, doesn't it? I broke my baby toe once. Rocked it in a rocking chair. Man, I couldn't believe how much that hurt, and for weeks."

"Since they put the cast on it has really calmed down, but it still aches." Claire adjusted the sling. "So what did you have to tell me? Let's get going."

Amy pulled out onto Highway 35 and told her story more slowly, describing the Swaggum's house and digging through the office, speeding up as she got deeper into her story, but this time Claire followed her and finally she got to the important piece of information: The Baldwins had hired Dean Swaggum to cut down a tree toward the end of June, less than two months ago.

"What do you think?" Amy asked.

"Seems like a pretty big coincidence. Two deaths, two murders possibly, happening within a week or two of each other and they had met less than two months previous. I think some pretty serious sniffing around needs to be done. Swaggum came down to this area to cut down a tree for the Baldwins. How do we find out what happened after that?" Claire asked out loud, then immediately thought of Colette, Anne's sister. Maybe she knew something. "I think you need to go back to Swaggum's wife and ask her if she remembers anything in particular about that job. I'm going to check in with Anne's sister. Oh, and why don't you pull the phone records for both the Swaggums and the Baldwins. See if anything shows up."

When they got to the department, Claire heard from one of the secretaries, Gwen, who had learned from Patsy, who worked at the mortuary, that Colette was trying to arrange for a small private memorial service at the funeral home. Not even in a church. To have a private ceremony of any kind was very unusual in Pepin County where often both weddings and funerals were announced to the general public in the paper, everyone welcome at either event.

But the bigger problem was that it wasn't clear if the sister had the legal authority to bury Anne Baldwin.

It was only a few minutes later that Colette stood in front of her desk. "They're telling me I can't bury my sister. They say that only Chet has the authority to do that. But where is he?"

Claire raised her unbroken hand and motioned for her to slow down. Her broken arm was starting to throb. "Sorry,

Colette, I don't think I can do anything to help you there. Chet hasn't turned up yet."

"I have every right to bury my sister. What if he never shows up? What then? What if he killed her? I'd like to throttle him, leaving her in the lurch like this." Colette seemed to realize for a moment where she was and who she was talking to. "Well, I just don't know what I might do."

Claire felt her arm throbbing faster, the tiny jolts of pain felt like torture. So did this woman's voice. "Let's step into the conference room where we can talk more privately."

Claire led the way to the small conference room down the hall. One big round table, chairs, no windows. Colette sat down. Claire sat right next to her. Maybe that way she would talk more.

Colette launched right in. "I can't stand the thought of Anne not being buried. It's just not right. I want to take her back to the farm and bury her beside our parents. I tried to get the funeral home to let me take over the arrangements of her burial but they say I don't have the authority. Can't you help me?"

Claire felt an unexpected wave of compassion for the woman. She didn't blame Colette for wanting to put her sister to rest.

"I'm sorry to say I don't think so. We haven't charged Chet with anything. He is still the legal guardian, the next of kin, for your sister and as such can make all the decisions."

"Well, where the hell is he?"

Claire felt like hanging her head, but instead she looked right at Colette and said, "That's my fault. I picked him up at the hospital and he ran away." Claire rubbed the slightly swollen fingers that were sticking out of her cast. "That's when this happened."

"Doesn't that prove how dangerous he is?"

"Not really. My broken arm wasn't exactly his fault."

"But his running away?"

"Yes, that's concerning us."

"Why haven't you found him? Why aren't you doing more? You know, get out the troops?"

"We have deputies out looking for him, but this is a small county and we just don't have the resources."

Colette deflated. Her shoulders slumped, her face sagged. She leaned forward and collapsed on the table, her head resting on her hands. "She's just lying there in the cold, waiting. This isn't right."

"I can promise nothing, but we hope to find Chet very soon and we will get this resolved." Claire needed to ask her some questions. "I found out that Anne was taking some medication for depression and also discovered that she was seeing a therapist. Did you know this?"

Colette puffed up again, sitting up tall. "Yes, she had told me about that. But so what?"

"Well, can you tell me why? What she was depressed about and why she was seeing the therapist?"

"I don't know everything. I mean, I didn't push her that hard to find out what was bothering her, but she would have told me if I had."

"What do you know?"

"I told you that things were difficult with her and Chet. She's been talking about that for a while. Concerned about how they were getting along. As I told you it seemed to have something to do with their sex life. You know he had surgery on his prostate."

"No, but I was wondering. He had some medication for prostate problems."

Colette wrinkled her forehead. "You know, don't all guys get that as they grow older?"

"Many of them do, but to varying degrees. How badly was it affecting Chet—do you know?"

"I don't know about that. But I do know…" Colette's voice broke and her shoulders shook. She clasped her hands together and looked like she was ready to plead with Claire. "I know that something bad had happened. Very bad. Anne wouldn't tell me what it was. She called one night about a week ago and was hysterical. She said that she couldn't stand herself. That she was a horrible person. That she didn't deserve to live."

Claire was stunned. Why hadn't Colette told her this before? No sense asking her that now. "Did she tell you why?"

"No. I tried to get her to, but she just wasn't talking straight. I thought she was drunk. Maybe it was those pills she started taking. I don't know. I couldn't get her to tell me what was wrong. When I asked her straight out, she hung up on me. I suppose I should have told you this before."

"Did you talk to her after that?"

"Yes, sure. I called her right back but she wouldn't answer the phone. When I called her the next day, she brushed it off.

She said she'd been having a hard day, no big deal. I couldn't get her to tell me anything more. I asked her what was the matter, but she shut up. I should have …" This time Colette started sobbing, the cries pouring out of her throat, shuddering through her whole body.

Claire reached out and put a hand on Colette's shaking shoulder. "You did all you could. You tried."

•   •   •

Rich sat at the kitchen table in the Baldwin's house and looked at the beer in his hand. Chet was a good friend. He wondered if they would ever drink a beer together again.

Rich knew he wasn't supposed to be in the house—Claire would have his head if she knew—but he had gone in to get some more dog food for Bentley. This afternoon Bentley had acted a little more territorial when Rich had gotten out of the truck, but then warmed up to him again. The poor guy must be missing Anne and Chet. Hard to be all alone, responsible for the whole farm.

After Rich found another bag of dog chow in the pantry, he had looked in the fridge—just an automatic gesture—and seen the six-pack of beer. He grabbed a beer, thinking how much he deserved it.

It was late in the afternoon, the hottest part of the day, and Rich was exhausted. He had slept very poorly on the couch last night. No matter what position he had put his body in, he hadn't been comfortable. Three nights of not sleeping in his own sweet bed were taking a toll on him.

The couch in the living room looked tempting, but he had work to do.

He took another cool swig of beer. He was mad at Claire and tired of being mad at her. Superwoman had to go to work. Certainly he wanted her to find out what had happened to Anne as much as anyone.

He was trying to figure out why he was so bothered lately. Yes, Claire had been difficult this summer, possibly because of sliding into menopause. Yes, he would have to be somewhat understanding of that. But somehow, he had never felt that she had fully committed to him, that she would trust him with her life.

It wasn't just the fact that they had never married. Although that did irk him. It was more how separate she could keep herself, how self-contained. He also knew that her first husband's death had damaged her and that the revenge she had taken had caused even more destruction in her soul. She deeply distrusted the world. She had looked evil in the eye and, unfortunately, saw it everywhere.

Rich had hoped she would get over that. He had hoped that years of being with a solid man who stood by her and fed her and loved her would make her believe in the basic goodness of people again. But he was losing faith that even all his love could change Claire.

Rich was no longer sure that Claire would ever give herself completely to him. He was afraid that she would always hold back a part of herself as protection.

He wasn't sure he could live that way with her.

That scared the shit out of him.

Rich finished the beer. When he bent over to throw the bottle in the trash under the sink, he heard the front door open.

CHAPTER 20

In the late afternoon, Jeremy drove Claire over to see Dr. Singh in Wabasha. The judge had come through with the court order, which was a piece of good luck. Court happened to be in session and the judge happened to be in a decent mood. Plus, Claire made a convincing argument—Anne's state of mind might make all the difference in a murder investigation.

Jeremy pointed out some of his favorite fishing spots as they drove the long causeway over the delta formed by the Chippewa River flowing into the Mississippi. Claire spotted some mallards paddling in the reeds of the slough, then through the trunks of the alders she saw the tall, angular form of a Great Blue Heron.

For a moment, she wished she could be in a small fishing boat in those quiet backwaters, staring at a bobber. Nothing on her mind, the heat bearing down on her like a comforting hand, a fish a possibility, but not necessary.

Then Jeremy asked, "How's your arm feel?"

She looked down at the fiberglass cast that covered her limb and said, "It's okay if I sit really still."

"That's hard to do."

"Impossible," Claire said.

Five minutes later, they parked in front of the clinic where Dr. Singh worked. "Jeremy, why don't you take a break? Go someplace cool, get a Coke, and come back in about a half an hour." Claire thought Dr. Singh might be more open with just one deputy asking her questions.

From her thin voice on the phone and her name, Claire had thought Dr. Singh would be small and Asian, but she was a tall, thin woman, with straight brown hair. If Claire had to guess her nationality she would have said German. Her blue eyes shone behind silver-rimmed glasses.

Claire introduced herself, handed Dr. Singh the court order, and waited while the woman perused it.

"Please come in." Dr. Singh opened a door to a very comfortably appointed room. A large oriental rug covered the floor, bookshelves rose floor to ceiling on one wall, and a large abstract painting in soft blues and greens filled most of another wall. Windows behind the desk looked out on a small garden.

Claire sat in a chair opposite the desk. Dr. Singh sat and folded her hands on top of her desk as if in prayer, or as if she was trying to keep them still. "I'm glad you've come. I thought about this all night and I've decided I needed to tell someone what I know."

"I'm so sorry about Anne Baldwin," Claire began. "I knew Anne fairly well, too."

"Oh, that's right. So you said." Dr. Singh sounded surprised. "I'm not sure if that makes me feel better or worse." Then, looking at Claire's arm, she asked, "What happened to you?"

"Just a tumble." Claire gave her a quick smile. "How long had Anne been seeing you?"

"Since early summer." Dr. Singh looked at her folded hands. "She was having problems with her husband. She was somewhat depressed and a bit anxious. Not an unusual combination."

"Can you be more specific?"

Dr. Singh shifted in her chair. "This is very uncomfortable for me. I'm usually the one asking the questions."

Claire said nothing.

"Her husband was having severe sexual dysfunction, to the point where they could no longer have sex. This made Anne feel like she was failing him somehow. Also she couldn't bear thinking that her sexual life was over."

Even though Claire had suspected this, it was hard to hear. "Was she thinking of leaving Chet?"

"Oh, no. That wasn't an issue at all. She loved him. But according to her, the sexual component of their life together had been very important to both of them and they were having a very hard time without it. Chet had even encouraged her to seek out other men, a suggestion that surprised her."

"Did she?"

Dr. Singh looked over at the painting. "Yes."

"With whom?"

"I don't know."

"Did Chet find out?"

Dr. Singh's face tightened. "I'm afraid so."

"What did he do?"

"This is so hard. I didn't know what to do. Nothing like this had ever happened to me before." Her hands pulled at each other in a worrying way.

"I have heard everything."

"I suppose, but maybe I should have done something." The therapist shook her head slowly and sadly. "I checked with a fellow therapist. The problem with reporting something like this is it's hearsay."

"It's not too late."

Dr. Singh spit out the words. "Yes, it is. It's way too late."

"What did Chet do?"

"I'm not sure. But I suspect the man died."

Claire couldn't believe what she was hearing. "Died? How?"

"I don't know. She didn't say."

"Anne told you this?"

"Sort of. One session, a little more than a week ago, she was hysterical. She said there had been an accident. Something about a man stopping by who had done some work for them. She said that Chet came home early and found them together. She said they were not in the house, but in a cabin. All she would tell me was that it was awful. That they fought. She said the man got hurt, but she wouldn't say anything else. I didn't know what to do."

This image of the scene stunned Claire. It must have happened in the cabin. They hadn't tested the cabin for blood or prints or anything. No reason to. It looked like the condom had not been used by Chet but by this other man.

"So you don't know what happened to the man? What they did?"

"She wouldn't tell me anything more. She left before the end of our session. Just walked out. I was so worried when she didn't show up this last week. I even tried to call her."

"Do you know what kind of work this man did?"

"She said he cut down a tree for them."

• • •

Usually Meg loved babysitting Rachel, but today the toddler had been fussy. She didn't want to take a nap, wouldn't eat much lunch, then pitched a tantrum when Meg wouldn't let her go for a walk. It was just too hot to be outside, and not much cooler in the house. Finally, Meg ran a cool bath and plopped Rachel in the tub. She filled the tub with toys and brought a chair in to the bathroom. Rachel had played in the water and Meg had read a book about a girl who has diabetes and thinks she's a vampire. The girl's situation made Meg feel better about her life.

Meg had just pulled Rachel out of the tub and toweled her off when she heard Bridget's car pull into the gravel driveway.

Bridget trudged up the walk, looking like she had had a hard day too. She pushed open the door, set her purse down on a chair, took Rachel from Meg's arms and said, "I think it's an eat-out night tonight. It's so hot in here. You should have taken her to your house."

"I thought of it, but we would have had to walk. I just couldn't do it."

"Don't blame you. What're you up to tonight?"

"Only one week left of vacation. Curt and I might go see a movie in Red Wing if anything good is playing."

"Can you stay for a minute? I haven't talked to you in an age. Let's go sit in the porch."

The porch was on the north side of the house, so slightly

cooler. With screens on three sides it caught any little breeze coming down the bluffs. Bridget and Rachel settled into the glider while Meg took a wicker chair.

Bridget continued. "A movie sounds nice and cool. So things are good with you and Curt?"

"Yeah, great." Meg was happy to sit and talk. She had been wanting to ask Bridget about some things she just couldn't bring up with her mom. "Bridget, how old were you when you had sex for the first time?"

Bridget shot her a look. "Where's this coming from? That's the kind of question you should be asking your mom."

"I did. I'm taking a survey."

"What'd she say?"

"She wouldn't tell me."

"Why do you think I will?"

"Don't turn into Mom on me. I'm just trying to figure this sex stuff out. I read books and it seems like everyone is having sex when they're like twelve."

"Well, I wasn't twelve. I was older than you."

"How much?"

"A couple years older. Relatively late even when I was a kid. But I don't regret that." Bridget blew on Rachel's sweaty forehead, then asked, "You need some contraceptives?"

"No, it's not that. Curt and I would be careful. It's just that he's the greatest guy. I mean, what if we don't have sex and then we break up and then I miss the chance to ever go all the way with him?"

"Believe me, there will be other guys lined up for that opportunity."

"You think I should wait?" Meg wished someone would be definite with her.

"What do you want to do?" Bridget asked her.

That was the problem—she didn't know. "I'm not sure."

"I'm not going to tell you what to do, but I will tell you this. Making out will never be as good as it is right now."

• • •

Jeremy dropped Claire off at the end of her driveway. As she walked up the slight slope, she still buzzed from all she had learned from Dr. Singh.

Her arm was killing her and she knew there was nothing more she could do tonight on the Baldwin case. First thing she would do is take one of her pain pills and sit in front of the air-conditioner.

She had called the sheriff from the road and told him what she had learned and then had set up a forensics team to meet her at the Baldwin's farm tomorrow morning. They would take the cabin apart and see what they could find there.

But tonight all she wanted to do was to stand in a cool shower, eat a decent meal, drink a cold beer and climb into bed, preferably with Rich by her side.

When Claire walked in the house, the only noise she heard was the air conditioner humming. Even though it was after six, there was no sign of Rich and no dinner on the table. Very unusual. She had never been much of a cook and, with her broken arm, didn't think she could manage even the simplest meal.

Good excuse to take him out to dinner. Burgers at the Fort sounded good to her.

She hollered, "Anybody home?"

No answer. A note was stuck to the refrigerator with a pheasant magnet: "Went to a movie with Curt. Be back by midnight. Your darling daughter."

The phone rang and Claire grabbed it with her good hand, hoping it would be Rich calling. "Hello."

"Claire, I checked out the phone records," Amy said.

"That was fast."

"Computers really speed things up. Anyways, not only were there a few phone calls from the Swaggums to the Baldwins after the date of the tree service, but this is what's weird: There was a phone call to the Baldwin's from the Swaggum's on the day that Anne died, late afternoon. After Dean was already dead."

"So it had to have been Mrs. Swaggum who was calling."

"That's what I figured."

"Have you checked this out?"

"Not yet. But I will."

"Okay. Let me know." Claire told Amy what she had learned from Dr. Singh.

When Claire got off the phone with Amy, she was so jangled she didn't know what to do with herself. She wished Rich were home.

The phone rang again as she was sitting next to it.

"Yeah," she answered.

Rich said, "Claire, get over here…"

The line went dead. She held out the receiver and looked at it as if it could tell her something more.

It had been Rich, telling her she needed to get over some-place. He must be at the Baldwin's. Maybe Chet was at the farm. And Rich was there.

Claire called the sheriff's department and told them where she was going. She grabbed the keys to her car. It was time to find out if she could drive with one hand.

CHAPTER 21

After parking a block away from the Baldwin's farm, Claire slid out of the car and started up the road, hoping that the dog wouldn't bellow out a greeting as she approached. She would just have to chance it. She wanted to sneak up on the house, because she didn't want to spook Chet. Rich had probably cut off their call because he didn't want Chet to know what he had done. Why else would the phone call have been cut off like that?

Rich's pickup was parked right by the barn. To calm herself down, Claire ran through a list of other reasons why their phone call might have been cut off: line problems, battery died, dropped phone. As she got closer to the house, she moved even more cautiously, watching her feet. At the bottom of the steps, she could hear voices in the house—Rich and Chet.

"…because of me," Chet was saying. "To put it bluntly, I couldn't get it up anymore."

Rich said, "But for god's sake, Chet, Anne didn't kill herself because you couldn't have sex anymore."

"You don't know," Chet answered, "It's more complicated than that. No one will believe what really happened. I know that."

Claire stepped up the stairs and was able to see into the kitchen. The two men sat on opposite sides of the small kitchen table.

"You can't know that. Let me call Claire again. We'll get her over here and you can tell her yourself."

Chet slammed back the chair he was sitting on. He stood up and waved something in his hand.

Claire could see that he had a gun.

"I don't want to talk to Claire. She won't believe a word I'm saying. Besides, I just don't care anymore." Chet's voice was loud and crazy with grief.

Claire stood very still. She had her gun holstered. She was hoping she would have no trouble managing it with one hand.

Rich wasn't reacting to Chet's outburst. He said calmly, "What do you want to do? I'll help you. Do you want to run away? Leave your home and your animals? Leave Anne unburied?"

"My Anne. She's all I want, all I've ever wanted. To be with her." Chet looked at the gun in his hand.

"Chet, sit down. Tell me what happened. Start there."

Chet pulled the chair back to the table and sat down.

"What happened the night Anne died?" Rich asked him. "You said you went for a walk."

Claire moved into the shadow of the door. She could still see the men and listen to what was being said, but she was sure she couldn't be seen. She slipped her gun out of its holster. Chet still had the gun in his hand, but it was resting on the table.

"Yeah, we had been fighting. Anne was really upset. She had been depressed for a few weeks, maybe longer. Hard to tell. Things were bad. I can't tell you how bad."

"Why? What was going on?"

Chet lifted up the gun and slammed the butt on the table. "I couldn't get it up anymore! I couldn't satisfy my wife. I didn't know what to do. So I left for about a half an hour."

"When you got home, was she dead?"

Chet shook his head, his voice breaking as he spoke again. "No, she wasn't. But she had the gun I gave her. She was standing in the living room, holding the loaded gun in her hand. Anne said she was going to kill herself. I didn't know what to do. She said some woman had called and asked about her husband, threatening her. She said she couldn't do it anymore. I tried to talk to her. I begged her to give me the gun. She let the gun hang loose in her hand and I was sure she was listening."

Sobs wrenched out of Chet like they were going to carry him away. He gulped and continued. "Then, she held up the gun. She stared at it. It was pointing right at her chest. I tried to grab it from her and she raised it up in the air. It went off. A blast. Then it all ended. The gun went off right in her face. My lovely wife. What I did to her."

"Chet, it wasn't your fault," Rich said.

Chet stood again. "You have no idea. No idea what this is all about. Because of me Anne started messing around with another guy. None of this would have happened if I hadn't become impotent."

Claire opened the screen door and stepped into the kitchen.

"Put the gun down, Chet," she said as clearly and as calmly as she could.

Chet swung the gun around, not aiming it anywhere. "I just want to be with Anne."

•   •   •

Everything went into a slow motion for Rich with two guns in the same room: Chet crazy and Claire on edge. He didn't want anyone to get hurt. He brought his hands up and set them on the table. "Claire, you need to back off."

Claire kept her eyes on Chet.

Rich was afraid of what she might do. He knew he couldn't stand it if she killed Chet. For once, she had to listen to him. "Claire, we can talk this out. It's going to be okay. Chet, put the gun down."

Chet's gun started to swing around. Rich knew what Claire was trained to do. "Stop," Rich yelled.

At the sound of his voice, Claire halted and looked at him, waiting for him to say something else. For once she was listening to him.

But Chet wasn't. His gun kept rising.

Rich tried to step in between the two of them as Chet pulled his gun in toward his body.

A shot sounded.

The wash of blood that swept Claire's shirt made Rich groan with horror. A deep wish that he could do anything to change what had just happened swept over him as he lunged toward Claire to catch her.

•   •   •

"I'm okay," she assured Rich. She wiped at the blood, wondering where it came from. "This isn't me. It's Chet."

Chet was on the floor, mouth open, eyes closed. Blood pumped from his chest, right under his collar bone. Claire heard a small sound come out of his mouth, like a mewl a hurt kitten might make. She dropped down on her knees next to Chet and checked his wound.

She looked up at Rich. "Get me a towel."

When he handed her a kitchen towel, she clamped it to Chet's chest and put her full one-handed weight on it. "Call the EMTs."

She could feel Chet breathing under her hand. "Come on, Chet. This is no way to go."

Chet opened his eyes. "I gotta tell you. I gotta tell you what happened. It doesn't matter anymore so you should know."

Claire knew that he probably wasn't going to die, the wound—while not quite superficial—was in a place that would do a lot of damage to his shoulder, but was not near any vital organs or arteries. But it was time for Chet to talk. "Yes, tell us."

"I hate to say it but—Anne killed him," he said. "I just want you to know I didn't do it."

"Killed who?" Claire asked, wondering what he was telling her.

"That Dean. I found them together. He and I started to fight. She shot him. Because she was afraid he was going to hurt me. She did it for me."

"Why'd you throw him in the river?"

"God only knows. Anne was worried what people would think of me, that they wouldn't let me be on the board any more. I was only thinking about her—how it would all come out that she had slept with this guy—when it was actually my doing, my fault. All my fault."

Claire looked up at Rich. He shook his head. How could two people think so crazy? Trying to protect each other, they blew their life apart.

"So you dumped him in the river?"

"Yeah, we weighed him down with a cement block. We thought he'd never be found. We thought no one knew that he had even come to our farm. Then the wife called last week and Anne fell apart."

Claire heard the ambulance's siren wailing up the bluffs. Chet didn't seem to hear the sound. His speech was slowing down, but he kept talking. "I loved her. It was all my fault. Didn't want anything to happen to her."

CHAPTER 22

On the Friday before Labor Day, two weeks after Chet Baldwin shot himself, Claire walked upstairs in the government center to the courtroom for his bail hearing. She sat behind him in the courtroom and could only see his face when he turned to talk to his lawyer.

Chet looked drawn, but she saw him give a crooked smile to his lawyer. He was still wearing a sling and bandages on his arm. He was also wearing ankle shackles, but he seemed more in the world again.

He was being charged with aiding and abetting the murder of Dean Swaggum. Mrs. Swaggum was also in the courtroom. She looked just as Amy had described her, like a lady from the fifties: white-blond hair, bright red lips, teary eyes.

After Amy had acquired the phone records of the Baldwins and the Swaggums, it had turned out that Mrs. Swaggum had called Anne on the day Anne had killed herself. Mrs. Swaggum had been looking for her husband and had gone down the list of people he had recently worked for. Her call must have petrified Anne.

Claire felt a hand on her arm and turned to see Rich settling into the seat next to her. He gave her a nod and she put her hand on top of his.

The District Attorney presented the charges and his recommendations to Judge Barker. "August first, Chet Baldwin came home to find his wife struggling in their cabin with Dean Swaggum. It appeared to Baldwin that his wife was fighting the man off, trying to get away from him and he wouldn't let her go. Baldwin pulled Swaggum away and they fought. Swaggum, being larger and younger than Baldwin, had the advantage. Mrs. Baldwin shot Swaggum, intending only to stop him, but the bullet caught him in the side and hit his liver. He died immediately.

"This version of the story has been corroborated by Anne Baldwin's sister, Colette Anderson. She claims that her sister had told her what had happened. That it was all her fault. Not quite two weeks later, Anne Baldwin used the same gun and killed herself. Forensics verifies that the same gun was used in both deaths. The bullet that killed Dean Swaggum was found in the cabin."

"Chet Baldwin did aid in the cover-up of the murder of Dean Swaggum, helping his wife hide the body in Lake Pepin. Because he made this confession while he thought he was dying, it is admissable in a court of law."

The judge addressed Chet Baldwin, "Would you agree with this summation? Is this how it happened?"

"Yes, your honor."

Claire found this exchange especially odd to watch because Judge Barker and Chet Baldwin had been friends for years and often went hunting together. Yet here they were in a court of law, acting as if they didn't know each other.

"Why did you dump the body in Lake Pepin? Why didn't you and your wife come forward with your story?" the judge asked.

Claire waited for Chet's answer. This was the question she had tried to snake out of his mind—what had he and Anne been thinking? Talk about a pointless murder leading to a pointless death. For nothing at all. If Anne and Chet would have come forward, they might have been charged with negligent homicide, but there was also a chance they would have gotten off—plus even if they would have been found guilty, it wouldn't have meant much prison time.

Chet cleared his throat. "Scared and ashamed, your honor. We weren't thinking clearly. Anne was scared that she would go to jail and I didn't want anything to happen to her. I didn't want anyone to know what we had done." Chet looked down and shrugged, then added, "Your honor."

The District Attorney continued, "Although at first Mr. Baldwin was not completely cooperative with the sheriff's department, I do not feel that he is a flight risk at the present time. His mental health has been in question, but he is currently taking an antidepressant and seeing a therapist. Dr. Donley, his therapist, feels that his mental health has stabilized."

With some emotion in his voice, the DA went on, "Chet Baldwin has been a member of this community all his life, more than that he has served on the board of commissioners for many years. He has a farm to take care of, animals that he must tend to. He needs to get back to his life. We are recommending a bail of not more than $50,000."

The judge nodded. "I do not need to consider this for a moment. Chet Baldwin has been an upstanding member of this community and we owe him a great deal. A tragedy has taken place in his life and he will have to face that in a court of law. But now I want him to go home and take care of his farm. I set bail at $50,000."

Claire was surprised that the judge had set it so low, next to nothing. She glanced over at Rich and he smiled with his eyes.

While Chet was in jail, Rich had come to see him every Sunday morning and every Wednesday night, the official visiting hours. He had taken care of Chet's farm and tended to his animals without complaint, but she knew he was ready to be done with all that. She also knew Rich had come today hoping to drive Chet back to his farm.

As they all stood, Rich leaned into her and whispered in her ear. "Bentley will be so happy to see Chet again."

●   ●   ●

Chet sat on the back steps of the house he had lived in all his life, watching the sun go down, Bentley stretched out at his feet like a dark shadow. His first day home and he had done all he wanted to do, left instructions for everyone. He didn't want to sleep in their bed without Anne. He didn't want to eat dinner without her. All he wanted was to be with her again. They had made some bad mistakes, but they had made them together. That's all there was to it.

Chet leaned over and stroked the dog's head. He was such a good dog. Could almost run the farm without Chet.

"Bentley, you want to go see Anne?" Chet asked.

The dog lifted his sweet brown eyes up to Chet's and whined.

"You'll see her soon enough, you old thing."

Chet thought of the last time he had seen Anne. She had been hysterical, sure that Dean's wife would go to the police and everything would come out about what they had done. Her face had been streaked with tears and she had screamed at him. He didn't want to remember her that way.

Chet let his head hang down between his shoulders, feeling the weight of it all. He had thought he would not lose her if she had some guy on the side, keeping her happy. He had pushed her to try to find someone she could have sex with. Some crazy idea he had about what she needed. Now he saw all she had wanted was his love.

So, for him, she had tried it, had a one-time fling with an easy-going guy who came to take a tree down for them. But she had hated it. The fact that she had slept with someone else made her feel dirty. When Dean came back, asking for more, she had resisted him. That's when Chet had come home and found them in the cabin.

Later, when he asked Anne why she had had the gun with her, she had said that she was scared of Dean. She thought he might pull something and she wanted to be sure she could persuade him to leave.

Too late to fix any of it, Chet thought. He stroked Bentley and lifted the gun to his head. The side of the temple seemed like a good spot to aim at, right by the ear.

He raised his eyes to the sky and they filled with tears, not of sorrow, but of sweetness. Only one person could make him want to leave this wonderful earth, only one woman. Unlike any other. Maybe she'd forgive him. As long as he was wishing, maybe in the afterlife he'd be able to make love to her again. That would be heaven.

Bentley whined at Chet, his eyes on the gun.

Good thing Bentley liked Colette. She would have her hands full taking care of the farm, but it would be good for her. Since she quit drinking, she needed something to keep her busy.

"It's okay, Bentley my boy. I know you'll be fine."

Chet had asked Rich to stop over in the morning. He was sorry that his friend would find the mess he was leaving behind, but not such a big mess anymore. He wished he could explain it all to Rich. But his friend would just have to figure it out for himself.

The last thing Chet saw was a bird rising up in the far meadow. He couldn't tell what kind of bird it was, but it flew toward him—its dark wings pulling through the air like delicate knives—and he knew it was time.

• • •

The heat had lifted. Instead of rising to over ninety degrees in late afternoon, it had stayed in the low eighties, the humidity dropped off to near normal. Claire sat on the deck to watch the sun set.

Curt and Meg blasted out the front door.

"We're going swimming," Meg announced.

The two lanky teenagers stood next to each other, brimming with all that was good about youth: energy, freshness and hope. Curt had on nothing but a pair of cut-offs, and Meg appeared to be wearing only a long pink t-shirt with a gold peace symbol printed on it. Claire assumed she had a swimsuit under the shirt.

"Glad to hear that. Wouldn't want you to run around town like that," Claire sat up to watch them leave. "Where are you going?"

"Just down to the lake."

They walked off and, halfway down the driveway, they grabbed hands and took off running.

Meg had talked to Claire a few nights ago about the decision she and Curt had made to hold off on having "full-blown sex" for at least a year. "It's been kind of a relief," Meg said. "Now we can relax for a while and just mess around."

Their decision was certainly a relief for Claire. Sex. She couldn't help thinking about all the problems it could cause: unwanted pregnancies, awful diseases, destruction of bodies and souls.

That morning Amy had told her she had broken up with Bill. She had hinted at some unacceptable behavior on his part, but Claire hadn't pushed it. She had never thought it was a good idea for those two to be going out anyway and she certainly didn't want to get involved in their problems. All she had said was, "Sorry. But now's the time for you to play the field."

Amy had laughed. "What field's that—the farm field?"

Claire looked up as Rich walked out the door onto the deck.

She felt a deep want for him rising up in her warm body. She was one lucky woman.

"You feeling okay about leaving Chet alone at his place?"

"Yeah, he seemed really calm when I dropped him off, almost happy I'd say. Gave me the feeling he was glad to be back there." He rubbed the top of her head. "How're you doing?"

"Perfect. You feel like taking a walk down to the lake?"

"A walk?" Rich rarely liked to go for a walk. But then he labored hard all day long, tending the pheasants, while she was usually stuck sitting behind a desk or in a car, driving around.

"Yeah, a stroll. It's such a beautiful night. The kids are going swimming in the lake."

"I don't think they need us guarding them."

"No, but how can we waste this sunset?"

He reached down to pull her up. "I have a better idea."

Living on both sides of the Mississippi River, Mary Logue writes children's literature, memoir, and has published three books of poetry. After publishing two stand-alone mysteries—*Red Lake of the Heart* and *Still Explosion*—she started the Claire Watkins series: *Blood Country, Dark Coulee, Glare Ice, Bone Harvest, Poison Heart,* and *Maiden Rock*. With Pete Hautman, she has also written the Edgar-nominated Bloodwater mystery series for children. Whether in Wisconsin or Minnesota, she makes her home with Pete and their two toy poodles, Rene and Jacques. Visit her at www.marylogue.com.